W9-BUU-071

ITACHI SHINDEN【暗夜篇】

NARUTO

ITACHI'S STORY

[M I D N I G H T]

Masashi Kishimoto
Takashi Yano

NARUTO ITACHI-SHINDEN ANYAHEN © 2015 by Masashi Kishimoto, Takashi Yano
All rights reserved.
First published in Japan in 2015 by SHUEISHA Inc., Tokyo.
English translation rights arranged by SHUEISHA Inc.

Cover and interior design by Shawn Carrico

Translation by Jocelyne Allen

No portion of this book may be reproduced or transmitted in any form or
by any means without written permission from the copyright holders.

Published by
VIZ Media, LLC
P.O. Box 77010
San Francisco, CA 94107

www.viz.com

Library of Congress Cataloging-in-Publication Data

Names: Kishimoto, Masashi, 1974- creator. | Yano, Takashi, 1976- author. |
    Allen, Jocelyne, 1974- translator.
Title: Naruto: Itachi's story : midnight / Masashi Kishimoto, Takashi Yano;
    translated by Jocelyne Allen.
Other titles: Itachi's story : midnight | Midnight
Description: San Francisco : VIZ Media LLC, [2016] | Series: Naruto true
    chronicles ; 1
Identifiers: LCCN 2016031721 | ISBN 9781421591308 (v1 paperback) |
ISBN 9781421591315 (v2 paperback)
Subjects: | BISAC: FICTION / Media Tie-In.
Classification: LCC PL872.5.I57 N36613 2016 | DDC 895.6/36--dc23
LC record available at https://lccn.loc.gov/2016031721

Printed in the U.S.A.

First printing, December 2016
Third printing, April 2019

ORIGINAL STORY BY
Masashi Kishimoto

TRANSLATED BY
Jocelyne Allen

WRITTEN BY
Takashi Yano

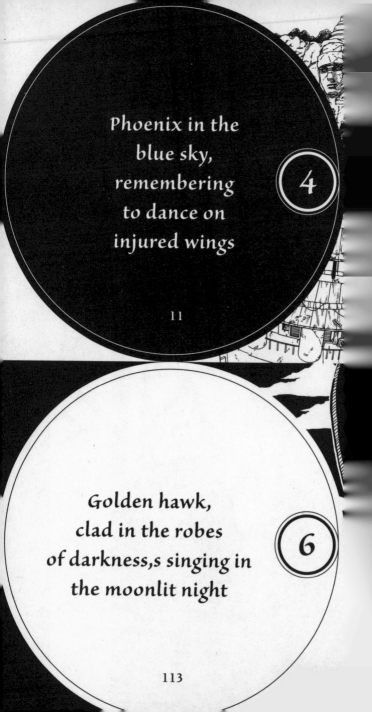

Phoenix in the
blue sky,
remembering
to dance on
injured wings

4

11

Golden hawk,
clad in the robes
of darkness,s singing in
the moonlit night

6

113

CONTENTS

The story thus far...

Rid the world of all fighting—the young Itachi is determined to make his dream come true. After graduating at the top of his class from the academy, becoming a genin, and gaining an early promotion to chunin, he aims to become the first Uchiha Hokage and races intently down a path to glory. Meanwhile, the rivalry between the Uchiha clan, originators of the Nine Tails incident, and the village increases in ferocity, and Itachi is pushed into joining the Anbu to be a bridge between the two. The condition for his entry is the assassination of the spy Kohinata Mukai, user of the Byakugan and Gentle Fist. Itachi's cruel fight, his despair, is beginning...

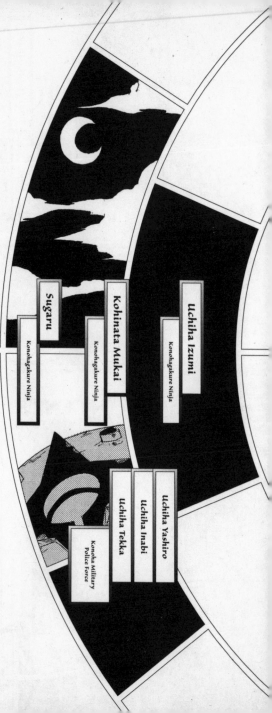

Sugaru
Konohagakure Ninja

Kohinata Mukai
Konohagakure Ninja

Uchiha Izumi
Konohagakure Ninja

Uchiha Yashiro
Uchiha Inabi
Uchiha Tekka
Konoha Military Police Force

CHARACTERS

Sarutobi Hiruzen
The Third Hokage

Shimura Danzo
Leader of the Anbu Foundation

Uchiha Itachi
Konohagakure Ninja

Uchiha Shisui
Konohagakure Ninja

Uchiha Fugaku
Father of Itachi and Sasuke
Head of the Konoha Military Police Force

Uchiha Sasuke
Itachi's Younger Brother

Uchiha Mikoto
Mother of Itachi and Sasuke

And no matter what you do
from here on out, know this.

I will love you always.

④

Phoenix in the blue sky,

remembering to dance

on injured wings

CHAPTER 4

Phoenix in the blue sky, remembering to dance on injured wings

1

Kohinata Mukai would be taking the following day off, his first in a month. Once Itachi learned this fact from the mouth of Shimura Danzo, he hardened his resolve.

The arrangements were soon made, and Itachi and Uchiha Shisui, who was to accompany him, had their duty schedules changed. Through Danzo's agency.

Itachi was going to kill a ninja living in his own village the following day...

Mukai might have been a traitor, but the fact that he was kin to Itachi was unchanged. He was a comrade from the village. It would have been a lie to say that Itachi wasn't reluctant to kill the man. But this mission was more critical than any he accepted thus far in his life as a ninja. He could not refuse.

Itachi kept very much in mind the fact that Mukai was a traitor. The man had been talking with Kirigakure in secret, and had leaked crucial confidential information about Konohagakure. Thinking about this helped Itachi set aside his feelings of guilt.

"Everything's ready!" A cheerful voice interrupted his med-itations. "Just like you told me, I put eight out there." His little brother smiled.

Itachi returned a grin.

They were in the middle of the woods. Now that he knew the mission would be completed the next day, Itachi was tak-ing a break, and Sasuke had begged him to join him for some training. In amongst the close-standing trees, Sasuke had hidden targets marked with double circles. And quite splendidly—Itachi couldn't see a single one of them.

"All right, Itachi," Sasuke urged him in a spirited tone, un-able to hide his excitement.

Nodding, Itachi grabbed his kunai. Once he had wedged one in between all his fingers, he had exactly eight in his hands. Eight iron claws sticking out from loose fists.

He lowered his face, and focused his mind just a little. He then poured the chakra built up in the depths of his stomach into his eyes.

Sharingan.

The breathing of the trees grew restless at once. In the rum-bling pulsation of writhing life, he saw small circular foreign ob-jects. Eight of them.

Itachi let out a small breath, and then he kicked lightly at the ground. In the air, his head and his feet traded places. With his body upside down, his center of gravity pointed downward and stretched out, stabilizing his posture. And stabilizing his pos-ture increased the precision of his control over his kunai.

He closed his eyes and imagined the eight targets in his mind. There were two that he couldn't reach from this position.

The one knocked over artlessly behind the front of the enormous rock was going to be the most trouble.

First, he threw the four blades in his left hand in a single motion. All unerringly pierced the four targets in relatively easy locations.

Next, the two kunai clutched between the thumb and middle finger of his right hand. These also dug into their intended targets without incident.

Two left.

Itachi's body was still in the air. Not even a second had passed since he leapt up from the ground.

He switched the kunai held between his middle and ring fingers to his left hand. Now he had one kunai in each hand. He waved both arms and threw the kunai at the same time.

The trajectories of the two blades overlapped. They collided in midair with a sharp *clang*, and then bounced off each other to fly off in unexpected directions.

He landed, his sharingan glowing with a crimson light.

As he stood up slowly, he felt the presence of his brother before him. Sasuke had hidden himself behind a tree to avoid danger, but now he popped his head out suddenly. He seemed dumbfounded at Itachi's skill in hitting all the targets. Sasuke's mouth hung open as he stared at the rock before him, the location of the most troublesome target.

Naturally, Itachi hit that one too. He had made the last two kunai collide, and changed their trajectories, to that end.

"Wow! You even nailed that target in the blind spot behind the rock!!" Sasuke flew out from behind the tree. He was clutching kunai in both hands. He was in such high spirits after that display of his big brother's skills that he was practically beside himself.

"All right! My turn!"

"Sasuke, we have to go."

Sasuke was practically pulsating with excitement, but he stopped abruptly. The face he turned toward his brother was thoroughly displeased. "You promised to teach me new shuriken techniques!" He glared at his brother in protest.

Itachi had indeed promised. But he had more than fulfilled that promise with what he had just shown the younger boy. "I've got a kind of important mission tomorrow. I have to get ready." Mostly mentally.

His little brother turned his face away and pouted. The cool eyes beneath the furrowed brow were twisted up as if he were about to burst into tears. "You're a liar, Itachi." Sasuke wasn't angry that Itachi hadn't taught him a new shuriken technique; he was angry because his time with his big brother had been cut short.

If possible, Itachi would have trained with Sasuke to his younger brother's heart's content. But the mission the next day was not a simple one. He couldn't neglect his preparations. He wanted to cry, too.

His little brother turned his face to the ground, even as he peered out at Itachi with resentful eyes.

Itachi waved him over, and the clouds on Sasuke's face were instantly cleared away. Happy footsteps ringing out in the forest, Sasuke raced over to him.

"Sorry, Sasuke. Another time," he said, as he popped his index finger up and poked his still-moving little brother in

the forehead.

"Ow!" Sasuke closed his eyes and cried out, his progress thwarted. He looked up at Itachi, his mouth turned downward on one side. Whenever Sasuke got this look on his face, Itachi knew he was planning something.

"Check this out!" Crossing both arms and readying his kunai, Sasuke smiled boldly. "Yaaaah!"

Before Itachi had the chance to stop him, Sasuke was flying toward the target.

"Hey! You're going to hurt yourself—" Itachi shouted, while before his eyes, Sasuke twisted his ankle, and plunged magnificently into the ground, headfirst.

∞

On the way home, carrying Sasuke after he hurt his ankle, Itachi walked toward the Uchiha compound in Konohagakure. Feeling the warmth of his brother on his back, the quiet time together passed peacefully.

Sasuke's aura sent out faint ripples. Itachi stopped, and looked at his younger brother over his shoulder. "What's wrong?"

"This is where Father works?"

"Konoha Military Police Force headquarters," Itachi answered his brother matter-of-factly, looking up at the massive concrete building, constructed with the circle as a keynote.

"This has been bothering me for a while," Sasuke continued, sounding rather grown-up. "Why is the Uchiha clan crest in the Military Police Force symbol?"

"You noticed that, huh?"

"Of course!" Sasuke replied, straightening up; Itachi's mouth naturally stretched into a smile.

"Right. Well, basically, our Uchiha ancestors organized and founded the Military Police Force. That's why they integrated our crest into the symbol for the organization. The Uchiha clan has handled and maintained public order in this village for a long time. The crest is proof of our proud history," Itachi explained, avoiding difficult words as best he could in his attempt to fulfill his brother's desire to learn anything and everything.

Sasuke listened silently.

"Right now, the Uchiha clan is smaller, but even now, basically all of us belong to the first squadron here, and contribute to maintaining public order in the village."

There were exceptions, like Shisui. Itachi had heard that the ninjas of the village had made an appeal, praising Shisui's superior talents. If Shisui were to join the Military Police Force, his interactions with ninjas outside the Military Police Force would have been severely curtailed, and he would have been completely contained within the Uchiha clan's framework. Due to entreaties from ninjas in the village who feared that outcome, Shisui had been assigned missions out in the field. However, Sasuke didn't need to hear all that, so Itachi abandoned that line of thought.

"The only ones capable of cracking down on ninja crime are even greater ninja." *And the only one capable of bringing to a close battles started by other ninjas is an even greater ninja.*

"Are you going to join too, Itachi?" Sasuke's innocent question pierced his heart.

I'm not. The real answer got stuck in his throat. "Dunno.

We'll have to see." He could never tell his little brother about joining the Anbu for the sake of their clan, and how dissatisfied they were with the village. All he could do was offer some non-committal response.

"Do it!" Sasuke shouted, in a voice free of worry, unaware of the dark circumstances of adulthood. His glittering purity wrenched Itachi's heart. "When I grow up, I'm gonna join the Military Police Force, too!!"

Both brothers in the Military Police Force, encouraging each other in their work. Days passing like a dream.

But that day will never come...

Itachi was going into the Anbu. And even if he lived in a world that would allow him to join the Military Police Force, he could never be content with that fate. His dream was to rid this world of war. The vessel of the Military Police Force was simply too small to realize something that big.

"Father's coming to my entrance ceremony tomorrow. It's the first big step toward my dream," Sasuke said. Itachi's baby brother's dream was to work as a ninja, together with his big brother, in the Military Police Force.

Itachi was glad. But that dream would never be realized.

"Yeah." The vague reply was all Itachi could give Sasuke.

∞

When they passed through the gates separating the Uchiha compound from the village, Itachi abruptly felt an aura beside the wall.

"You're late. What were you up to? I want to talk to you."

Their father, Fugaku, arms folded in front of him, was looking at Itachi. "Let's get home."

"Yes, Father," Itachi nodded.

Their father started walking straight toward their house with a confident stride, and Itachi moved heavy feet to chase after him, his little brother still on his back. When had he become annoyed at facing his father like this?

He knew the answer. But he didn't want to acknowledge it.

∞

His father's room. Their father sat with his arms crossed before Itachi and Sasuke, sitting alongside each other. "I'm told it's tomorrow," Fugaku said abruptly.

Itachi stayed silent, feeling his heart start to pound in his chest. He knew what his father meant. Fugaku was talking about the assassination of Mukai the following day. That was what was making Itachi's heart beat faster.

Exactly how much does my father know? And who did he hear about the mission from?

Itachi had a vague answer to the latter question. It had to be someone close to Danzo. But why had Danzo leaked information about the mission to his father?

Doubt called up more doubt, stirring up Itachi's heart.

"Ha, ha. That's my boy. It's only been six months since your promotion to chunin, and you've already come so far."

Itachi looked at his father silently, and Sasuke turned worried eyes on his older brother.

"Tomorrow is a special mission…and I've decided to go along."

Itachi's heart pounded more fiercely than it had all day. But the rocking of his brother's heart next to him was many times fiercer.

Their father's head was filled with the clan, and he had forgotten exactly how important the next day was for his younger son. Anger toward his father welled up in Itachi.

"If you succeed in this mission, Itachi, your entry into the Anbu is basically secured." Fugaku looked at his silent son, his eyes dyed crimson. "You know that, yes?"

Itachi was only allowed to take one person on the Mukai assassination. He had also already told Danzo that Shisui would be that one person. The fact that his father didn't know this meant that he didn't know the particulars of the mission. He had likely only been told the day the mission was to be carried out.

Fugaku despised the village, and here he was being toyed with, via information brought in from the village. His father seemed so pitiable to him, Itachi could hardly stand it.

A mission that required him to be ready to die. It had to be Shisui by his side. He would not allow his father's interference.

"You don't have to worry so much. Besides..." Itachi looked at Sasuke. Even though he was likely on the verge of bursting out into loud sobs, his wise little brother was pushing back his own feelings and smiling.

"It's all right, Itachi..." He felt as though he could hear Sasuke's voice in his head.

A smile spread across Itachi's lips, and he put his words into his eyes. *"Tell him... Tomorrow is a big day for you, right?"* He gave the smaller boy a push with the power in his eyes.

"Dad...Tomorrow is my—"

"Tomorrow's mission is a very important one for the Uchiha clan!"

His little brother's courage was shattered by the hard words of their father, his mind focused on nothing but the clan. Sasuke lowered his head, a frozen look on his face, as he desperately held back his tears.

Itachi's anger toward his father surpassed his limits. Was the clan *that* important? Did he not care about Sasuke?

All that Itachi saw in his father's eyes was the future of the clan. The man hadn't given a single thought to the fact that his elder son was about to go on a possibly fatal mission. And he didn't even see his younger son. How could he ever win against Konohagakure with such a narrow outlook?

Itachi hated all of it.

"You know, I'm not going on the mission tomorrow, after all," Itachi said.

"Have you lost your mind?! You know how important tomorrow is! What on earth are you saying?!"

"I'm going to Sasuke's entrance ceremony at the academy tomorrow."

His father caught his breath. At that moment, for the first time, Fugaku remembered what Sasuke was doing the following day. This, too, made Itachi so angry, he could hardly stand it. It was sad.

"It's customary for relatives to attend. You must have gotten the notice...Father." Itachi was serious when he said he was abandoning the mission. Those words came from the bottom of his heart, and were no lie.

His father tried to understand this. After a fleeting silence

CHAPTER 4

flowed through the room, he let out an exasperated sigh. "All right. Enough. I'll go to the academy."

Fugaku then stood and walked toward the dinner table, where their mother was waiting. Itachi and Sasuke followed him out of the room. From the garden came the dry sound of the bamboo rocker arm of the *shishi-odoshi* clacking against the stone.

Itachi knew that now that he had said all that, his father would absolutely go to Sasuke's entrance ceremony. His son's entry into the Anbu was the first step toward realizing the dearest wishes of the clan. He couldn't make a mess of it over Sasuke's entrance ceremony.

It was precisely because Itachi couldn't have his father come along on the mission that he had seriously intended to go to Sasuke's entrance ceremony. And being sick and tired of everything, wanting to go to the academy, none of that was a lie, either. But still, he couldn't actually give up on accomplishing the mission with Shisui.

Joining the Anbu was not a foothold to realizing the dreams of his clan. It was a modest step toward realizing his own dream of becoming the most skilled ninja in the world in order to get rid of all fighting. He had no intention of giving up on that.

And to that end, he had used his little brother. He despaired of himself.

Although it had been decided that their father would take part in the entrance ceremony after all, Sasuke seemed to feel responsible for the stormy air between Itachi and Fugaku, and he trailed quietly behind his older brother.

Itachi looked at him over his shoulder, and hiding his

own feelings of guilt, he said, "Make sure you really ice that ankle." Did his face stiffen up as he smiled when he said that? He hoped not.

"All right," his younger brother replied, a complicated look on his face.

Itachi had no idea what to say to Sasuke at that moment.

2

"It's no exaggeration to say that I live for that kid," Kohinata Mukai said, blowing cigarette smoke out into the air, while Itachi held his breath before him. In the hand not holding the cigarette, Mukai clutched a silver bottle of sake.

The three ninjas stood looking at each other, surrounded by more than ten Kirigakure ninja sprawled out on the ground, unconscious. They had all been defeated by Itachi and Shisui alone.

"Surrender quietly, Kohinata Mukai," Shisui said, from beside Itachi. The comma-shaped marks of the sharingan had already popped up in his eyes. "The Hokage is lenient on those who turn themselves in. He probably won't kill you."

Hanging his head to avoid those sharingan, Mukai let an ironic smile slip across his face. "Shisui of the Body Flicker, I mean, you're a well-known ninja. But still, well, I always got the impression you only walked in places where the sun hits. Or..." He stopped suddenly, and drank from the silver bottle. "...is it that you're still just a kid?"

Mukai opened only his right eye, and sneered. His con-

descending attitude forced a line to carve itself out between Shisui's eyebrows. "You know what I've done. So you should know whether or not I'd be allowed to turn myself in." A flick of Mukai's thumb, and ashes fell from his cigarette. "That I would get for my assassins the two prodigies of the Uchiha clan, at the height of their popularity, is truly the greatest honor."

He tossed his cigarette in the portable ashtray he pulled out of his pouch, and then put the cap on the silver bottle, before tucking it away in the pocket of his vest. "Real serious situation here," he murmured, his chakra suddenly increasing dramatically.

His Shadow Clones had returned. When Mukai's chakra grew in volume, Itachi released his own Shadow Clone, standing watch at Konoha Hospital.

"Now that he knows the dad he was talking to 'til just a minute ago was a Shadow Clone, my son's prob'ly angry." Mukai glared at the two ninjas in front of him as he scratched his head. "Now I'm gonna have to make some kind of excuses when I get home." He dropped his hips low, and readied himself with his palms at chest-height, in the manner particular to Gentle Fist.

"Why would a ninja as good as you be a spy?" Itachi spat out the feelings in his heart.

"When you get old, things happen. You can't understand what those things are until you get some years on you. So even if I did tell you why, you'd only get half of it."

"If you die, what happens to your son in the hospital?"

"Because of those things I mentioned, I can't be dying here. Even if you guys were to kill me." Countless lines raced out from Mukai's left eye all around him.

"Byakugan!" Itachi shouted, but Shisui was already flying backwards to get some distance from Mukai.

"I can't go easy on you. Forgive me." Mukai's voice reached Itachi's ears.

At once, the distance between them closed. With incredible speed, right and left palms came flying toward Itachi's throat and solar plexus simultaneously.

When Mukai's sword hand stabbed into Itachi's stomach, reaching for his solar plexus, Mukai bent his index and middle fingers inside Itachi's body.

"Hah!" Mukai spat out a breath that was a battle cry, and his sword hand yanked out Itachi's intestines.

Instantly, the Itachi standing there with his guts ripped out transformed into an overwhelming number of crows, and danced upward. Rather than try to avoid the beaks attacking him, Mukai endured it with an elegant turn of the head, as though nothing were happening.

Shisui was creeping up behind him. "Fire Style! Great Fireball Technique!" He quickly wove the signs, and a ball of fire large enough to swallow Mukai shot out of his mouth.

Mukai faced the ball of flames dead on, still standing with the palm of his right hand thrust out in front of his face.

Direct hit.

No.

The ball of flames split perfectly into two in front of him.

It didn't look like he had executed some kind of jutsu. And it wasn't as though his body were cloaked in some kind of special aura. To Itachi, it was like the ball of flames itself had decided to split on its own in front of the man.

"Gentle Fist cuts off enemy chakra. Using it means being very familiar with that flow. Jutsu are the embodiment of chakra. If you can read the flow, it's not so tough to split it," Mukai explained with a grin, and raced toward Shisui.

Shisui's face darkened. Even if he did have above-average physical jutsus, his opponent was a user of Gentle Fist, a technique far beyond the level of a physical jutsu. It was no wonder Shisui looked gloomy.

Itachi watched from a distance on high as the battle unfolded.

Inside the domain of the Land of Fire, three or so hours to the north of Konohagakure, the three ninjas were fighting in a small basin surrounded by slightly elevated mountains. Not a single blade of grass grew on the rocky mountains, and there were any number of places for a lone person to hide. Itachi had slipped behind a convenient rock, and was watching over the other two as they fought.

It had only been his Shadow Clone up against Mukai. Itachi hadn't moved from this place since the fight started.

Their opponent was a user of Gentle Fist. It was almost too difficult to strike the killing blow in close combat. This contest would be decided by a single long-distance blow.

Sharingan was a visual jutsu. Users put their own chakra into their eyes, and ensnared opponents in the jutsu. In other words, as long as Itachi could see the fight, he could ensnare his enemy in the jutsu.

Eyes meeting was not something that happened only subconsciously. Expecting no particular trouble, an enemy would let their gaze race around the scene. As long as that optical axis and the optical axis of the jutsu user were in alignment, it was possible to create a situation in which the enemy's gaze would intersect with the jutsu user's, without the enemy's even being aware of it.

Itachi was waiting for that moment. And to that end, Shisui had dared to take on dangerous close-range combat, trying his best to get Mukai in alignment with Itachi's optical axis.

If Itachi could just activate the visual jutsu of the sharingan, they could make this work. If they managed to pry open one small seam in Mukai's mind, Itachi could use that as a foothold, and gradually push his visual jutsu to encroach ever further. The problem was that first step.

In addition to his vast experience, Mukai was a user of the byakugan, a kekkei genkai that allowed the flow of chakra to be sensed visually; naturally, he understood what the sharingan was, and could do. Itachi and Shisui had adopted this strategy to break down those tall walls.

Just barely dodging Mukai's left thrust, Shisui threw his torso back. Given the perfect opportunity, Mukai pressed in on the younger man.

Shisui leapt backward, as if in flight. In that instant, Mukai's face was turned toward the rock Itachi was hiding behind. But their optical axes still had not intersected.

Mukai turned his gaze toward Shisui as he landed, and then abruptly averted his eyes.

The sharingan had been activated.

Naturally, Shisui's sharingan had been a feint. The place toward which Mukai had turned his face was in the exact direction of the rock concealing Itachi.

Itachi's gaze, his mind sharply focused on his enemy, and Mukai's gaze, unconsciously taking Itachi in, intersected.

Or they should have.

When they were a hair's breadth apart, Mukai kicked suddenly at the ground and flew upward. An incredible leap. When he landed, he kicked at another rock, and bounded into the sky again.

Itachi's hiding spot had been found out.

In the previous instant, Mukai had noticed Itachi's presence with the power of the byakugan. He had probably also understood in that moment that Itachi's sharingan had been activated.

Perhaps to confirm his own hunch, or perhaps to draw Itachi out into the fight—either way, Mukai was leaping straight toward the rock where Itachi was hiding. Itachi didn't fail to notice Shisui standing behind him, grinning, before his friend disappeared.

Shisui next appeared in front of Mukai.

"Tch!" Clicking his tongue, Mukai was knocked back into the rock wall rising up perpendicularly, as Shisui's kick ripped into his face. His skull split open.

Or so Itachi thought, before his eyes took in a splintered log. "Shadow Clone!" he cried out.

"Right..." He heard Mukai behind him.

Gentle Fist stance.

"Eight Trigrams Two Palms." The heels of his right and left palms slammed into Itachi's stomach in succession.

"Eight Trigrams Four Palms." Before Itachi had a chance to breathe, this time, four blows slammed into him.

"Eight Trigrams Eight Palms." As if sneering at Itachi's brain as it fumbled for the start of a counterattack, Mukai assaulted him mercilessly with successive attacks.

"Ngaaaaah!" Itachi heard a cry from Mukai's right side. The byakugan's blind spot.

In the corner of Itachi's hazy field of view, Shisui launched a flying kick.

"Shisui…" Itachi had the leeway to murmur his friend's name, because Mukai had dropped into a defensive posture.

No. The word "defensive" was too simple. As Mukai dodged the kick merely by angling his head, he grabbed hold of Shisui's neck with his outstretched left hand, and held him up high, lifting the sturdy body of the young man with a single arm.

Strangled like this, Shisui struggled frantically. But the five fingers sunk into his throat simply would not peel away.

"There's this thing called 'training' that you do to overcome your weak points. The first step in my training was to compensate for the byakugan's blind spot in one eye, with physical jutsu. Don't underestimate this old man, brats."

"Kohinata Mukai…" Unconsciously, Itachi called the name of the powerful enemy before him. His feet had also taken a step forward without him realizing it.

"What? You want me to kill him?"

It was easy to see why he'd think that. Beaten hard by Gentle Fist, the flow of chakra in his body interrupted, what kind of counterattack could Itachi have left? Moving forward without any kind of plan was basically an act of masochism.

However, Itachi's feet would not stop moving. Even though he didn't remember telling them to do so, they continued to walk artlessly toward Mukai.

"Then I'll put him out of his misery, as requested!"

"Hngh!"

The hand around Shisui's throat tightened its grip. Mukai was going to crush his Adam's apple.

"Stop!" Itachi shouted, and the sharingan in his eyes glittered.

"There's no way that sort of obvious genjutsu is going to work on me," Mukai said, turning his face away from Itachi.

Before the man's eyes was Itachi's friend's face.

"Mangekyo sharingan," Shisui murmured. The eyes of his friend, now crimson, took on a shape unlike any other sharingan Itachi had ever seen.

Normally, the sharingan had a small black dot in the center of the eye, and in the circle around that, the snake tails of *magatama*-shaped specks popped up. The power differed depending on the number of magatamas, but the form itself was common to the entire clan.

But Shisui's was different. The three commas of the magatama were enlarged and connected, and the small black dot in the center had disappeared, leaving a crimson hollow. If the ratio of red to black in a normal sharingan was eight to two, then Shisui's eyes at that moment appeared to be a fifty-fifty struggle for supremacy.

Most likely, the intersection of the gazes of Shisui and Mukai had lasted less than a thousandth of a second.

For a normal sharingan, the user couldn't be certain of capturing his opponent in a moment that short. Shisui had not missed that fleeting instant. Mukai had definitely been ensnared in the genjutsu.

"Mukai!" Shisui shouted, dumbfounded, the hand around his throat releasing him at last. Before his eyes, Mukai fell, a spray of blood shooting from his stomach.

Itachi stared, rooted to the spot.

Mukai had cut his own stomach. The instant Shisui's sharingan had been activated, Mukai had stiffened slightly, and pulled a kunai from his pocket to slash a cross into his own belly.

"Hold on, Mukai!" Shisui shouted, crouching down to cradle the ninja's head.

"I'm a spy for another village. Any interference with my brain, and a jutsu that makes me end my own life is executed. You can't save me." Mukai coughed, and blood spilled out of his mouth. "I-I've never seen anyone caught in a genjutsu in that short a time before... What the hell was that?"

Shisui didn't answer.

"Uchiha secret jutsu, huh?"

Shisui faltered, and Itachi glanced at him before addressing Mukai. "Do you have anything you want to say?"

"S-so, this is where we're at... I did what I did on my own. My wife and kid had nothing to do with it..."

"So, you're saying the crime of treason was yours alone?"

"Totally selfish, but, well..." With a trembling hand, Mukai groped for something in his pocket.

Itachi pushed aside Mukai's fingers, and pulled out the object he was fumbling for. He grabbed a cigarette from the package, and put it between the man's lips.

"L-light..."

This time, Shisui pulled the lighter from Mukai's pocket, and held the flame to the end of the cigarette.

Mukai took a long drag, letting the smoke flow down to the bottom of his lungs, before exhaling the smoke as though relishing the taste.

"This is how a ninja dies, you know? I'll be waiting for you over there..." Mukai's hand dropped, cigarette still between his fingers, and he stopped moving.

"It's over," Shisui said, his voice shaking with exhaustion.

Itachi nodded. "That sharingan..."

"Will you keep quiet about it to the guys in the village?" Shisui murmured, still staring at Mukai.

"Yeah."

"Mangekyo sharingan," Shisui said, and his eyes showed once again the strange pattern. "When the time comes, I'll tell you—just you—everything."

Itachi felt an irresistible attraction to the unknown power secreted away in his friend.

3

"Team Ro, hm?" Danzo muttered, gaze trained on the paper before him as Itachi stood at attention and watched.

They were in Danzo's room of the house given to the Foundation. Sitting in front of the ebony desk, Danzo rested the elbow of his left arm on the armrest, and held the papers in his right hand, not even glancing at Itachi.

"The team leader is Hatake Kakashi, hm?"

"Yes," Itachi replied, briefly. He had been curious this whole time about the man standing beside Danzo.

A Foundation member in a white tiger mask. It wasn't anything particular about the man or the mask. He was just curious. The eyes on the other side of the round holes in the white mask had been staring at Itachi, almost glaring at him. For some reason, the treacherous gaze unsettled him.

"He is an excellent ninja," Danzo said, almost a declaration.

Hatake Kakashi…

Itachi had been saved by him not long after he became a ninja. On a mission to guard the daimyo of the Land of Fire, they were attacked by an unknown man, and Itachi's teammate Tenma had been killed. His sharingan not yet awakened, Itachi had been prepared for death, faced with the overwhelming difference in power between himself and the man.

However, the man had suddenly muttered Kakashi's name, and vanished. Even now, Itachi didn't really understand why the man had disappeared. Just that he had definitely murmured Kakashi's name, and vanished. But Itachi had no way of knowing now if it was because the man was afraid of Kakashi, or if it was for some other reason.

"He has a darkness inside. This is the most important element for the Anbu."

Darkness… Do I have that too? Itachi questioned himself.

"Rest assured. You also have plenty of darkness," Danzo said, almost as though he had seen right through Itachi. Having come into contact with Danzo any number of times now, Itachi wasn't particularly surprised. The man excelled at discerning other people's mental states; it was a simple thing to jump ahead with suppositions to a certain extent, and reply to unspoken

thoughts. That was all Danzo was doing.

"Prepare a transfer celebration," Danzo said, dropping the paper and standing up. He tucked his ebony chair under the desk of the same material, stood next to Tiger Mask, and looked at Itachi. And then he placed a hand on the man's shoulder, and a rare sunny smile spread across his face. "This man is going to be on loan to Team Ro."

Although Danzo's Foundation was also a part of the Anbu, it had a different chain of command and leadership from the Anbu, which was under the direct control of the third Hokage; the two organizations were completely separate. Itachi had heard that because of this, they didn't regularly exchange information or personnel.

"Don't worry. I naturally obtained Hiruzen's permission," Danzo offered, as if reading his mind once more. No matter how many times that Itachi heard that arrogant way of speaking, he could never grow to like it.

"NICE TO MEET YOU. MY NAME IS SUGARU," the man in the tiger mask abruptly said. His voice was mixed with a dry rustling sound, as if something was stuck in his throat, making it hard to hear what he was saying.

"Sugaru had a serious illness in his throat when he was young, and he hasn't been able to speak that well since."

"MISSIONS WHICH REQUIRE TALKING ARE DIFFICULT, BUT OTHER THAN THAT, I WILL DO ANYTHING." There was a strange quality to his voice, but his tone was light. He seemed to have a friendly nature.

"You can use this man as your hands and feet."

"Hands and feet?"

"YES," Sugaru replied to Itachi's question to Danzo. "I AM A

MEMBER OF THE FOUNDATION. MASTER DANZO'S ORDERS ARE ABSOLUTE. SO, IF I AM ORDERED TO BE THE HANDS AND FEET OF ITACHI, I AM PREPARED TO GIVE MY LIFE FOR YOU, EVEN IF YOU ARE YOUNGER THAN ME," he noted, with a deadpan look that implied sarcasm.

Itachi didn't even smile as he stared at Danzo. "I can make it in the Anbu by myself."

"Don't take this too seriously. At best, Sugaru is on loan to Team Ro. Your team leader Kakashi doesn't know about this. And you needn't even be aware of Sugaru. But he will always be keeping you safe."

"Keeping me safe? Are you saying that someone is targeting me?"

"The first Uchiha Anbu, a mere eleven years old. That position's plenty to inspire prejudice and jealousy."

Itachi was silent. He had indeed been baptized by the kunai of his comrades on the road from the training ground that was the venue for the meet-and-greet with Team Ro. It wasn't as though any of them had hit him, but kunai had come raining down on him endlessly from the air. A wordless force to block his path to the training ground. Itachi hadn't avoided them or protested, but simply walked through them indifferently.

After realizing what his comrades had done, Kakashi had scolded them, but there wasn't one person who was really sorry for what they'd done.

"I value you. I won't have you dying young because of the jealousy of your teammates, or some such."

"No matter who attacks me—"

"Do not underestimate the ninjas of the Anbu." Danzo cut Itachi off. "The closer you get to the center of the village, the

more people you will encounter who do not have a favorable impression of the Uchiha. It's entirely plausible that some of them might try to kill you, and make it look like you died during a mission. And if you died, what would your clan think?"

"Impossible..."

"I'm saying that that impossible situation is entirely possible." Danzo nodded deeply, as if to affirm Itachi's thinking.

Itachi dies on a mission. His father and the others suspect a plot on the part of the villagers. Itachi's death would be the perfect trigger for an explosion, for those dissatisfied with the position of the clan within the village. When Itachi thought about the fact that his own death could become the trigger for a coup d'état, he felt a shiver run up his spine.

"You're already in a position of serious responsibility with both the Uchiha clan and in the village." Danzo moved away from Sugaru, and came around the desk to stand next to Itachi, before placing a gentle hand on his shoulder. "You must be a bridge connecting the village and the clan for me. Live a long time, Itachi."

Danzo said the same sort of things his father had said.

Konohagakure and the Uchiha clan...

Was this a relationship of equals?

The Uchiha clan were also people living in the village of Konohagakure. In which case, wasn't the antagonistic nature of their relationship unnatural right from the start? Why didn't Konoha have complete rule over the Uchiha clan? Why did the clan harbor such dissatisfaction toward the village, despite the fact that the brethren of the clan had even been given the right to self-governance?

A presence to connect the two. As his father put it, a pipeline. In Danzo's words, a bridge. They were the same thing.

"I will protect you. You fulfill your duties in the Anbu without worry, Uchiha Itachi," Danzo told him smugly.

Itachi bowed slightly, before quickly leaving the room.

∞

"It's been a while, huh?" Izumi said, her head hanging.

Itachi was in a small park in the clan compound in the evening. He had joined the Anbu without incident, and finished his report to Danzo. At the entrance to the compound, he had run into Izumi, on her way home from a mission. Without either of them inviting the other, they naturally turned toward the park. Izumi got on a swing, while Itachi sat down on the bench behind her.

"Sorry about that time."

"That time?" Itachi asked in response.

Izumi looked back at him over her shoulder, as she swung back and forth. "You know, at the tea shop in the village."

He remembered. Izumi was apologizing for getting mad and flying out of the shop.

They hadn't actually talked—just the two of them—since then. All kinds of things had happened in the intervening days, and Itachi honestly hadn't had the time to think about her. So, he had completely forgotten about the incident in the tea shop until that very minute.

To start with, though, even if she was apologizing now, Itachi hadn't been angry at all at the time, so it wasn't as though

he had anything to forgive her for.

"I'm the one who should apologize," Itachi said.

"Why would you have to apologize, Itachi?"

"I didn't think it was bothering you that much."

"Ha, ha!" Izumi faced forward again, and pumped harder on the swing.

"What?"

"I was just thinking that's so like you," she said in a bright voice, seemingly in a better mood now. Her feelings shifted so abruptly that Itachi couldn't keep up.

Not wanting to take her off this cheerful track, he tried to change the subject. "How was your mission?"

"No big deal compared with you," she said, and kicked at the swing to fly up into the air. She did a somersault, and landed beautifully. Spreading out her slender arms, Izumi turned around. "They just use me however I'm handy, like taking care of the daimyo's wife's pets, or helping move the Land of Fire admin to a new office, and stuff."

"That's it, huh?" Itachi's mouth naturally spread into a smile. He was relieved that she hadn't been on any dangerous missions. He deliberately tried not to look at the answer to the question of why he was relieved.

Itachi himself thought he was still half a person as a ninja. Which is why he didn't have the mental leeway to think seriously about Izumi.

"Walking down the same path as the person you like... Maybe I shouldn't want that."

He had understood Izumi's feelings when she said that before running off. But he couldn't respond to them.

"Hey, Itachi?"

"What?"

"If... so just like, what if, all right? If you hadn't become a ninja, what would you be?"

"I never thought about it." Itachi had been born to ninja parents, and he had never had any doubts about becoming a ninja himself. He believed that only ninjas could gain the power required to realize his dream of ridding this world of war. So, he was unable to think of a path other than becoming a ninja.

"You haven't?" Izumi hung her head sadly. "I heard you joined the Anbu."

"You did?"

"Everyone in the compound knows."

The Anbu was a deeply secretive division. The village also wished that the ninjas who belonged to it would not make themselves known, to the extent that that was possible. And yet, Itachi's posting to the Anbu was already spreading throughout the compound. The idea that this showed the strength of the solidarity of the clan was a nice one, but was it really all right for so much information to be leaked? The clan were so quick to mention a coup-d'état—what would they do if the people in the village were to hear of it?

"Hey, Itachi?" Izumi's voice brought him back to reality. "I'm scared."

"Of what?"

"I feel like you're getting further and further away."

He felt something touch his chest suddenly. Izumi's head rested there, below his own. "I-Izumi..."

"I-I'm sorry, Itachi. But just let me stay like this a little longer."

Unable to do anything else, Itachi simply waited for Izumi to calm down again.

"We're still eleven years old. But, Itachi, you're already... Where are you going, Itachi?"

"I'm not going anywhere."

Probably... He swallowed that last word.

4

"A little anticlimatic, isn't it?" the man in the fox mask asked, standing next to the simple door opposite Itachi as if to keep the door between them. When Itachi stayed silent, the man added, "Well, just because it's the Anbu doesn't mean it's all dangerous missions. Guarding the Hokage is a legitimate mission, too."

"I know that," Itachi replied, matter-of-factly. Like the man, his face was covered with a fox mask. In contrast with the almond eyes of the man's mask, however, the holes that opened up in the position of Itachi's eyes were round.

The name of the man in the mask with the almond eyes was Hatake Kakashi. He was the leader of Anbu Team Ro, and Itachi's direct supervisor. Although he was still young, at twenty years old, he had already been a member of the village's elite Anbu for eight years. He was talented, and the Hokage trusted him implicitly. Itachi had known about him for a while.

The time Tenma died...

It was this very Kakashi who had come to help Itachi. And if he had shown up a little sooner, Tenma might not have died.

Ninjas focused only on reality and results. The fact that Tenma was dead was something that could not be reversed. Itachi had no intention, at this late date, of thinking about these sorts of "what-ifs," and layering on the reproaches.

"You remember the basic tactics of the Anbu?" Kakashi lobbed an innocuous question his way. He was a good supervisor, carefully considering the feelings of his young new subordinate.

Friend-killer.

The phrase of choice for people looking to badmouth Kakashi. Itachi had heard it any number of times since he joined the Anbu.

However, every time, it had been from someone older than Kakashi satisfied with their subordinates. It was nothing more than an insult stemming from annoyance or jealousy.

"If it was to complete the mission, Team Leader Kakashi would even kill his friends." The faces of those uttering this ugly abuse were always mean.

But on a day-to-day basis, Itachi had never heard a single world against their comrades from Kakashi. In fact, it was actually notable how careful he was to pay his respect to the bonds he shared with them. At that very moment, Kakashi was being extra attentive to Itachi, who had only just joined the Anbu; he was intently searching for a way to start a conversation.

"I've got the basics in my head," Itachi noted, standing straight, and not looking at his kind team leader.

"No surprise there."

For Itachi, who had read every document he could get ahold of on the use of small ninja teams, the particular strategies of the Anbu were extremely fascinating. Four-person teams, three-per-

son teams, two-person teams. Even what action to take as a solitary ninja. The list of practical tactics—from constant offensive positioning, to exploring the possibilities for the completion of the mission—was comprehensive, including every situation a ninja might encounter on a mission. Everything from feints and disturbances to defensive formations and cooperation had been honed and specialized to crush the enemy and execute the mission. Spurred on by his intellectual curiosity, Itachi had devoured the thick Anbu tactical books in a single night.

"There's clearly a reason why they called you a prodigy when you came to the academy," Kakashi said.

"I'm not sure if the youngest graduate ever can really say anything here."

"When I graduated, it was in the middle of the Great War, and they needed ninjas. The situation's different now."

Now that Kakashi mentioned it, the current system at the academy was different from how it had been when Itachi graduated. The Great War and its aftereffects still lingered when he graduated. Because of that, once his actual abilities were recognized, he was skipped ahead, leading to his early graduation. But now that it was a time of peace, the Hokage was determined that ninjas must be carefully cultivated over a number of years, and it was no longer possible to graduate in a short time, as it had been in the past. Thus, no matter how talented Sasuke was, he couldn't become a ninja until he was eleven years old.

"It's only in my head. Once I actually try moving with my comrades, I won't be able to say that I studied anything."

"You'll be fine," Kakashi said, almost as though he had seen it already. In his voice, Itachi heard no excessive expectation or irresponsibility from carelessness or pride. His voice was completely casual. Which was exactly why it was mysteriously persuasive. "I'm hoping that the Anbu will become a place of pride for you."

"Thank you."

A supervisor I can count on... There was something about this man Kakashi that made him think that.

∞

No matter how many times I come here, I never grow to like it...

In the main building of the shrine, dominated by heat, Itachi took a deep breath through his nose. Filling the space all around him were the brethren of the clan.

The regular meeting.

Now that Izumi was a genin, she was there, too. Since she was the same age as he was, and because he was still a novice, Itachi was in a lower seat in the same row as her, separated by a few people. Perhaps overwhelmed by the heat, she was still, her face lowered. He wanted to call out to her, but with the heat, and the main building actually falling silent at that moment, there was a wordless pressure that would not allow him to do anything so rash as that.

"Well, then, let's begin." His father stood up from his seat in the front row, and turned toward everyone gathered in the hall. Those present held their breath, and waited for Fugaku to speak. The scene was like the founder of some religious sect and his believers.

The leader, burdened with the resentment of the clan... This was

the dark face of Itachi's father, Fugaku.

"It has been officially decided that my son Itachi will join the Anbu. He has already begun to carry out missions as a member."

A quiet cheer echoed through the shrine.

"Now we have a pipeline connecting our clan with the center of the village. No longer will we simply receive from the village; we will also actively investigate, ourselves."

It wouldn't be his father doing that.

"Itachi," Fugaku called his son's name.

Without a sound, Itachi got to his feet, and waited for his father to speak again.

"You have joined the Anbu. Have you noticed anything?"

The question was much too vague, confusing Itachi. The villagers were prejudiced against the clan, and did not think well of them. That was likely the answer his father was hoping for. And in fact, his comrades in the Anbu had not celebrated Itachi joining them; there were even some who made a show of their displeasure. But he couldn't say without reservations that this was simply because he was a member of the Uchiha clan. At eleven years of age, Itachi's youth was another source of irritation.

"It is a fact that the people of the village are wary of the Uchiha clan, and do not think well of us," Itachi began.

"It is!" Once Itachi offered the answer his father was seeking, a sympathetic voice called out from the seats.

"But," Itachi continued, giving his voice extra weight as if to push back the hasty hooting, "that said, I don't feel any active hatred, no persecution of the clan. At best, I believe their feelings are the sort of worries and jealousies that anyone has."

As his father listened with arms crossed, only his right eyebrow twitched upward. "This worry and jealousy you mention can come together, and be twisted into a bigger emotion."

As if to agree with his father, the brethren began to chatter, and make a commotion.

To push through the voices of the crowd, Itachi concentrated his strength in the bottom of his belly, and spat out, "If you add on backward predictions like that, anything can be reduced to a negative phenomenon!"

As if to stand in the way of his father, silently glaring at him, a single man stood up. His father's trusted retainer, Yashiro.

"Hey, Itachi!" he called, his narrow eyes gleaming murderously. Silently, Itachi turned to his father's confidant. "You're really siding with the village here, aren't you? Whose ally are you anyway, the village's, or the clan's? Maybe your judgment's a bit dull after joining the Anbu—getting a little full of yourself?"

"It's better not to force things into a framework with words," Itachi murmured.

"What?" Yashiro called back.

"Enemy. Ally." Itachi's eyes shone a faint crimson. "If you differentiate between things with the tool of words, you lose sight of the true situation. You're forced to step into places you shouldn't."

"I don't have time for this incomprehensible back and forth. Whose ally are you, Uchiha Itachi?!" Yashiro's angry roar returned the main shrine to silence.

"It's obvious, isn't it?" Itachi glared at his father's retainer. "I am a member of the Uchiha clan."

∞

"You got a sec?" Shisui called out.

The meeting over, Itachi was walking home a little ways behind his father. Fugaku looked back, curious at Itachi's suddenly stopping, and saw his son's good friend there. "What's wrong, Shisui?"

"I wanted to talk with your son for a minute."

Fugaku looked at Shisui and Itachi in turn, before saying simply, "Don't be too late," and walking off into the night by himself.

"Shisui." Itachi said his friend's name once they were alone together.

"I understand how you feel so well, it hurts." His friend's brow furrowed, and he looked vexed from the bottom of his heart. "Yashiro's the leader of the group pushing for a coup. To that man, all the people of the village are enemies."

The abuse Itachi had been showered with earlier still echoed in his ears. He lowered his face, as if to look away from the image of Yashiro that rose up in the back of his mind.

"Since it looked like you were going into the Anbu, I did some maneuvering of my own."

"What do you mean?"

"I talked directly with the Hokage, and obtained the authority to independently investigate the true state of affairs in the clan."

What did investigating the true state of affairs in the clan mean? Itachi was confused, not immediately understanding what his friend was saying; Shisui opened his mouth again, as if understanding that.

"I've been taken off my regular duties, to make sure the clan doesn't get any more riled up. Their dissatisfaction is going to explode. The Hokage promised that I could act at my own discretion to prevent that, and gave me a position in the Anbu. But that's just in name only. In the end, I report directly to the Hokage, so your dad and the others don't know about my joining the Anbu. Even inside, only a few people know."

"You actually went to the Lord Hokage?"

"Relax. I didn't say anything about the coup."

If the village found out about the clan's scheming, Itachi could see that they would no longer be able to continue as they had up to that point, with each keeping the other in check.

"Itachi, we're gonna keep fighting to stop the clan from exploding. You from inside the Anbu, and me as a ninja, reporting directly to the Lord Hokage."

"No matter what happens, I'll never forget my promise with you."

Shisui thrust a fist out. Itachi stuck his own out to touch it. "Above all else, we have to make them stop with the coup, at least," Shisui said firmly.

Itachi nodded in agreement.

5

Itachi didn't want to believe what he saw before his eyes.

In a windowless room in the basement of the building given

to the Anbu, monitors were crowded together, their screens full of sights familiar to Itachi.

"The Nine Tails incident. The village officials suspected Uchiha involvement," Kakashi remarked, standing beside him.

Itachi listened, staring at the monitors.

"Not satisfied with just isolating the clan compound on the edge of the village, they started monitoring everything in the compound, twenty-four seven."

"And that's this room?"

"It is."

His Anbu comrades were controlling the images with the countless buttons and levers in front of the monitors. He couldn't see the expressions on their faces because of the masks they wore, but despite this, he felt fairly certain that they were relaxed. That was the extent to which his comrades had let down their guard. And no wonder. For them, this was a monotonous job, simply staring at monitors. They didn't give a thought to how monumental it was for the Uchiha clan.

"So, we can see everything?"

"We don't need to check on each and every little thing, but basically."

"I understand. I will under no circumstances inform the clan."

There was no way he *could* tell them. If they found out that every corner of the compound was being monitored twenty-four hours a day, the rage his father and the others felt would become even more intense. It would simply add ample fuel to the fire for those who were clamoring for a coup.

Itachi had been sent to the Anbu by his father as a spy to

investigate the true state of affairs in the village. If he were to faithfully fulfill that role, he should report this fact to the clan immediately. The moment he abandoned the idea of telling them, he abandoned the idea that he was a clan spy.

"From now on, you're going to be monitoring here all day."

"You're telling me to watch my clan comrades?"

Abruptly, the man in the monkey mask, who had been sitting in front of the monitors, listening quietly to the exchange between Kakashi and Itachi, stood up. "Whether they're your clan comrades or not, a mission is a mission. Your clan drew in sNine Tails. So they're being monitored. Accept reality, newbie."

"Kou." Kakashi spoke the name of the man in the mask reprovingly.

Their colleague next to Kou whirled around in his chair, and turned his mask toward Kakashi. It was the round face of a cat. "His little sister was killed by the Nine Tails. So he doesn't have the best impression of the Uchiha clan."

"Don't involve your personal feelings in a mission," Kakashi told them.

"I understand. I'm sorry." Kou came closer, head hanging. He bowed neatly, and passed by Kakashi. "All right, you're up, newbie," he said, unhappily.

The round face of the cat trailed after him.

"Oh, you're here, good," Kakashi said, looking at the door the two men had disappeared through.

Standing in front of it was the ninja who had been with Danzo, Sugaru.

It had already been just over four hours since Kakashi left. Sugaru had not said a single word. Itachi had never been

CHAPTER 4

particularly good at small talk anyway, so he didn't find the silence painful. The time simply passed, with the two of them staring intently at the monitors.

It was pure chance that he saw it.

Although it was his mission, Itachi's blood was not cold enough to allow him to coolly watch over the lives of his brethren. He frequently switched the monitor image before his eyes, trying as much as possible not to stay in one place. By viewing a series of moments like this, he managed to maintain his presence of mind somehow. He had trained to memorize a scene with a single glance, so Itachi was confident that he was amply executing his professional duties.

At one of these momentary fragments, he felt the faintest sense that something was off, and he stopped his hand.

The composition he expected, from the gates of Nakano Shrine. The stone paving of the path stretched straight out from the stone gates to the main building of the shrine. But the space precisely in the middle, between the gates and the main building, looked slightly twisted to Itachi's eyes. Just for a fraction of a second.

The scene in the monitor had already regained its stillness. It had been a faint disturbance that Sugaru most likely hadn't noticed. If anyone else had seen it, they would no doubt have thought it was simply the wind shaking the camera.

But Itachi had seen that disturbance before. The scene near the center of the stone paving had been disturbed by a vortex centered on one point. Almost like the surrounding space was being sucked into that point.

The man in the mask...

The phenomenon shown on the monitor was exactly the same as the jutsu the man in the mask had used when he escaped after he attacked Itachi and his team, during the mission to guard the daimyo of the Land of Fire.

"Why would that man…" Itachi muttered carelessly, before he noticed Sugaru's presence, and regretted it. But Sugaru's attention was focused on the monitor before him.

Annoyed by his own inexperience, Itachi dove once more into the sea of his thoughts.

When Tenma died, Itachi had clearly seen the right eye of the man, shining behind the mask. A black dot floated in the center of a crimson eye, three comma-shaped magatamas in the concentric circles. He was certain that the man's right eye had been a sharingan. Which meant that he was a member of the Uchiha clan.

Over three years had passed since that incident. From time to time, the scene of his teammate's death would come back to life in his mind. Tenma lost his life, an almost unsightly terror plastered on his face, looking as though he had no idea what was actually happening. Itachi had been astonished at the overwhelming difference in power that existed between himself and the man in the mask. He had despaired at his own powerlessness, and ended up activating his own sharingan. All of which meant that the man in the mask was the man who had awakened Itachi as a true Uchiha ninja.

The murderer of his colleague, and yet, a person he was indebted to. He felt a strange connection with the man in the mask.

Over the last three years, Itachi had wondered any number

of times about the man's true identity. From what he could infer, Itachi had thought the man was perhaps a member of the Uchiha clan, but that changed to a certainty now.

The blur in the video was because of the man in the mask. The man had appeared at Nakano Shrine. The day Tenma died, a sharingan had glittered beneath the attacker's mask. All of this clearly pointed to him being a member of the Uchiha clan. So then, who exactly in the clan was it?

In the ensuing three years, Itachi had had contact with all the men of the clan living in the village. There was no one with ninjutsu to control space the way the man did. There was also no one with that same voice or aura. And more than anything else, Itachi had a hunch that the man was not someone from the village.

So then, who?

The Uchiha clan had lived in the village of Konohagakure since its founding. And he hadn't heard of anyone outside the Uchiha clan having the sharingan. Although there were exceptions like Hatake Kakashi, they were still within Konohagakure. If precious kekkei genkai like the sharingan or the byakugan had been leaked outside the village, it would have been a serious affair for the entire nation. There was no way the village records wouldn't have mentioned it. And as of the present date, there was nothing about the sharingan being leaked to another village.

When he thought about it like this, the possibilities naturally narrowed. The first was that a member of the Uchiha clan thought to have died in the Great War had survived, and become the man in the mask. It was a general rule that if a member of the Uchiha clan died in battle, their sharingan would be brought home by another ninja. So, the man couldn't have stolen it from a corpse. In which case, it made sense to assume that someone thought to have died was alive, and coming to the compound with his sharingan still in his possession.

The second possibility was that the man in the mask was someone who had broken away from the Uchiha clan. This was less likely than the first option. Because since the founding of Konoha, only one person had ever broken away from the clan and left the village.

Uchiha Madara…

The man who founded Konohagakure together with Hashirama of the Senju clan. He had left the village, and was said to have died in battle with Hashirama in a place called the Valley of the End.

It wasn't possible for someone who had died to be alive. At this point, Itachi should have abandoned this second option. But for some reason, he couldn't completely put it aside. He had felt the man's overwhelming chakra, his powerful presence, for himself, and it had been stronger than that of any ninja Itachi had encountered up to that point.

If a ninja like that had died in battle, then it should have gone down in history. However, nowhere in the records of the great battles of the past was the death of such a capable Uchiha ninja verified.

In which case…

Itachi could consider the idea that Madara was alive.

"…TACHI." A voice came at him from far away.

"ITACHI!" Sugaru called Itachi back to reality. "It's about time to switch shifts."

"Mm," Itachi answered vaguely. Even as he had indulged in his thoughts, his fingertip had kept pressing the button. Although he was not watching it at all, the monitor he had his eyes trained on changed from one scene to another in quick succession.

"ARE YOU ALL RIGHT?"

"What do you mean?" he asked in response.

"No...IT'S NOTHING." Sugaru didn't say anything more.

6

About two months had passed since Itachi joined the Anbu, but his monotonous days continued unchanged. His main duties were guarding the Hokage's office and practicing with his comrades; he still hadn't been given any missions that would expose his life to danger.

"You couldn't exactly say the village was at peace if we were out on assassinations and dangerous missions all the time. The fact that we've got nothing to do is proof of peace," Kakashi had said, and laughed easily.

The village is at peace...

And yet, Itachi wondered. If the village was supposed to be at peace, then why was his heart in such turmoil? Why did he feel like things were so urgent?

Because of his clan. In the shadow of the tranquility of the village, the Uchiha brethren were seeking chaos. This was the main cause of the disquiet in Itachi's heart.

Whatever happened, he had to at least prevent a coup. But he couldn't come up with a concrete plan to do that. He had said he would move with Shisui, but the two of them could stand side by side with their arms spread out, and they still wouldn't be able to completely hold back the clan's eagerness for destruction. The fact that he couldn't find a way to break this deadlock had Itachi panicked.

"Wah, ha, ha, ha!"

An earsplittingly loud voice pierced his ears on his way home from work. Unconsciously, his feet stopped, and he noted the little park ahead of him. It was already late in the day, evening. The sun had long ago slid off to the west, and a gloom was descending on the area.

A boy, likely the one who laughed, was standing on a swing, staring out at three human shadows running off. Probably his friends.

"I'm telling you, you guys don't have a chance against the great Uzumaki Naruto here!" the boy on the swing shouted.

The shadows didn't turn back toward him, but left the area, chatting to each other about something, seemingly friendly with each other. Staring after the three, the boy who had named himself as Naruto sat down sadly on the swing. His earlier words had clearly been a show of courage. Itachi had understood this, once the boy named himself.

There was no one in the village who did not know Uzumaki Naruto.

The boy before him had been involved in the Nine Tails incident that had terrified the people of the village. The child with the Nine Tails inside him. When he walked along the road, ev-

eryone lowered their voices. There was only one person who did not know that the Nine Tails lived within his body.

That was Naruto himself.

He was unaware of the calamity in the village; it was sealed up in his body, and he lived with people in fear of him. Naruto couldn't understand why people persecuted him. And both of his parents were already gone from this world. He had no one to shower him with unconditional love.

Itachi turned his feet toward the park. He advanced quietly toward the swing with the boy, moving weakly back and forth. He sat down beside Naruto, whose face was turned to the ground.

"Whoa!" Noticing Itachi's sudden appearance, Naruto nearly fell off his swing in surprise. He flapped his arms and legs more than absolutely necessary, and managed to stop the swing before turning suspicious eyes on Itachi. "Don't go scarin' me like that."

"Sorry."

"So, like, who are you?" Naruto stared at him with wide eyes.

Pumping the swing, Itachi turned his gaze forward. "It doesn't matter who I am, does it?"

"My mom says I'm not s'posed to talk to strangers."

"She's gone, though?" Itachi said.

A bashful smile spread across Naruto's face as he threw his right hand up to the back of his head. "So, you know that?"

"Uzumaki Naruto is a famed prankster."

"Am I that famous?"

"In a certain sense."

"Heh, heh, heh!" Naruto laughed happily, unable to

understand Itachi's sarcasm.

"Your friends ran off."

"If they don't get my pranks, then they're not my pals." Naruto's voice was excessively bright, like he was trying desperately to act cheerful so that his loneliness wouldn't be seen.

Everyone knew Naruto's true self.

For the village, the Nine Tails incident had left a scar deeper than any other. Suspected of having controlled the Nine Tails, the Uchiha clan was also still trapped under that cloud. Itachi himself had been slandered more times than he could remember because of it. There was probably not a single person in the village willing to have any meaningful contact with the boy who housed the source of that trauma in his body.

In other words, Naruto was the greatest victim of the Nine Tails incident.

Itachi didn't know how the Nine Tails came to be sealed in the boy's body. But he thought that anyone who would seal the embodiment of disaster in a baby was not in their right mind. Perhaps they hadn't considered how the child would be persecuted.

The details of the Nine Tails incident were a closely guarded secret in the village. The truth was hidden in darkness, and only Naruto was left. Naruto was one part of the darkness of the village. The village had been built sacrificing people like Naruto. The village officials had sealed the disaster in Naruto, and directed the dissatisfaction of the people somewhere else with their persecution of the Uchiha clan, in order to skillfully keep the village running.

Deliberately producing a darkness to hide their own darkness...

And now Itachi, too, was one part of the darkness in the village. Because the Anbu itself was the true darkness of the village.

"Bro!"

"Hm?"

Naruto widened his eyes next to him. "You just got real quiet all of a sudden. You all right?"

"I'm fine."

"All right, good." Naruto looked up at him, with worry in his eyes.

"It's probably time for you to be getting home."

"I can go home, but it's not like there's anyone there." Naruto's mouth twisting downward, he put on a show of being tough.

"Then I'll go home."

"What?!" Naruto cried in exaggerated surprise when Itachi stood up.

"Keep fighting," Itachi said, words he thought offered no real peace of mind.

But Naruto seemed happy, and chuckled to himself as he rubbed his nose with a finger. And then he leapt forcefully off the swing, stood tall, and pointed his index finger at Itachi. "My name's Uzumaki Naruto! I'm gonna be Hokage someday!"

"You are? Hokage, huh?" A flame blazed up in Itachi's heart. Even as he carried the burden of the village's darkness, this boy was not giving up on his own destiny. Not resenting the village, not hating the people, he believed in his own dream, honestly and wholeheartedly. "I hope you are."

"I'm totally going to be Hokage. Remember me 'til then, Bro."

Smiling in response, Itachi turned his back to Naruto, and started walking.

The heavens above glittered with stars.

∞

Danzo called him in. He sat in his chair with a sour look on his face. Next to the master of the Foundation was Sugaru, supposedly a member of Team Ro. "How's the Anbu?"

"I don't know yet."

"An honest answer. You'll no doubt have any number of experiences from now on that you could only have in the Anbu. Until then, polish your skills," Danzo said, almost as if he were Itachi's boss.

But Itachi was in the Anbu, which was under the direct control of the Hokage, with no connection with the Foundation. In terms of work, Danzo and Itachi basically had nothing to do with one another.

"I called you here today for a reason."

Itachi nodded silently.

"I've heard that the Uchiha clan compound has been particularly strict with outsiders lately."

It was true that in the last few months, the compound had taken on an air of exclusivity. It seemed that his father giving voice to the word "coup" had given the compound itself a will.

"You are also going to the regular meetings?" Danzo asked, point-blank.

The Uchiha clan was monitored twenty-four hours a day by

the Anbu. It was only natural that Danzo would be aware of the meetings.

"Yes," Itachi answered honestly, preparing himself for the worst, knowing that there was no point in hiding anything.

Danzo nodded deeply, seemingly satisfied. "I'll be frank. I want you to report the details of those meetings to me." His voice slammed into Itachi, containing indescribable pressure. "If things continue as they are, the Uchiha clan will fall. Your power is needed to stop that from happening."

"Are you telling me to betray my clan?"

"You're not betraying them. You're saving them." Danzo rested his elbows on his desk and set his chin in intertwined hands. The hollow of his left eye, a deep, dark cavern, peered out at Itachi. "Betrayal is an act that brings about a disadvantage to the betrayed. The act of reporting the details of the meetings to me is to prevent the explosion of your clan, and as such, it is advantageous to them. Thus, it cannot be said to be betrayal."

A neat bit of rhetoric.

Danzo likely intended to complicate his thinking and blind him, but Itachi was not fooled. No matter what the result was for his clan, telling Danzo what happened at the meetings was nothing other than betrayal.

Danzo had misread him. Itachi was not fixated on the word "betrayal."

"I understand."

"Given that you hate fighting more than anyone, I thought you might say that," the master of the Foundation said, in a voice that did not reveal his emotions.

Itachi hated it, but it was just as Danzo said. He still hadn't been able to come up with a concrete plan to stop the coup d'état. Danzo's request, coming at such a time, had an irresistible appeal.

They had been able to gain the cooperation of the third Hokage, thanks to Shisui. And Itachi's decision here might turn into an opportunity to use Danzo's power. He would prevent his clan's implosion by connecting it with the center of the village.

"I don't want to do anything to rob your clan of dignity. I leave the selection of information you bring to me to you."

"Thank you."

"I'm counting on you, Itachi. The fate of your clan rests on your decisions." Danzo's voice weighed heavily on Itachi.

But Itachi's resolve was not so weak that it could not withstand that weight. He took a deep breath, deep enough to reach the pit of his stomach, as if realizing the heavy responsibility he had been saddled with.

It smells like blood somehow...

Stricken raven,

faced with the death of a comrade,

deciding

CHAPTER 5

Stricken raven, faced with the death of a comrade, deciding

1

"So this is how it's going to be, huh?" Kakashi muttered.

Beside him, Itachi held his breath. At that moment, his team leader, the lower half of his face covered by a black mask, was already gone. Itachi jumped off the cliff after him.

The dead bodies of his comrades lay in the valley ahead. Land of Frost ninjas had killed them.

The two lands had been on the verge of forming an alliance when it happened. The alliance was to be made official ten days later, and they had been in the middle of a mission to exchange letters stating the final terms, when the ninjas from the Land of Frost suddenly bared their teeth.

The enemy had been uninterested in an alliance from the start.

Four Konoha ninjas up against ten from the Land of Frost. Outnumbered. In the blink of an eye, the Konoha ninjas tasked with the duty of receiving the letter had been killed.

If they witnessed the breakdown of negotiations, they were to exterminate the enemy: that was the mission Itachi and his team had been given. In other words, they were not to move until the situation was clear. Thus, their initial response had been delayed, leading to the annihilation of their allies.

The moment ten Land of Frost ninjas appeared—a suspiciously large force—it had felt very much like a breakdown in the process. If the Anbu had leapt out at that point in time, their comrades might not have died. However, even if Itachi had been leading the team, he couldn't have moved until all four were wiped out.

Ahead of him, Kakashi landed in the midst of the enemy, his right hand already piercing one of the ninjas. A stream of blue lightning enveloped his arm.

Chidori... Kakashi's best technique.

By the time his team leader was pulling his arm back out, Itachi had landed dead center among the enemy.

There were two other Anbu with them. One was Sugaru. And the other was a ninja called Tenzo. He was a little younger than Kakashi, but his career in the Anbu had already been fairly long.

"Konoha Anbu!" an enemy ninja shouted.

In the next instant, a thick tree branch tangled up around the man's throat and tightened, like a snake. Unable to push back against the incredible force of it, the man expired, long tongue lolling from his mouth.

It was Tenzo's jutsu. He was able to use Wood Style, a ninjutsu only the first Hokage, Hashirama, had been able to use.

"Konoha never had any intention of making an alliance with us, hm?" another enemy said to Kakashi.

"You came at us first." Kakashi didn't wait for the other man to argue the fact; Chidori dug into the other ninja's stomach.

Itachi heard a shriek from behind him. Looking over his shoulder, he saw an enemy hurtling toward him, a long sword held up above his head.

Itachi turned around. The sword closed in on the top of his head. He quickly lifted his arm, and grabbed the wrist of the enemy's hand on the hilt.

"Ngh!"

"Give it up," Itachi advised, still clutching the man's wrist.

Unable to bring the sword down on Itachi, the enemy glared at him, cold sweat popping up on his forehead.

The sharingan.

His enemy shuddered violently once, and then completely relaxed. Like a marionette with its strings cut, the man had started to droop and fall toward the ground, when his head rolled off into space before Itachi's eyes.

A ninja blade glittered to the rear of the enemy. Sugaru.

"THE MISSION FROM THE LORD HOKAGE IS THE EXTERMINATION OF THE ENEMY," Sugaru murmured in a voice only loud enough for Itachi to hear. He had seen through Itachi's secret plan to trap the man in genjutsu with the sharingan, and make him pass out.

There was no need to exterminate the enemy. Whether their envoys returned or not, the incident here would soon be known to the Land of Frost. It was vengeance enough to take out the ones who had murdered the four Konoha ninjas. Letting the others live, and return home to relate the true power of Konoha, would be a more effective check against the Land of Frost.

"I know," he told Sugaru's back, as the man was already turning toward a new enemy; then, Itachi set his sights on a new target.

There were four enemy ninjas left. They had already lost the will to fight.

Sugaru's blade flew toward the neck of one on his knees, begging for his life. Beyond him, Tenzo's Wood Style ninjutsu produced sharp branches that pierced the back of a female ninja trying to flee.

"This will make the Land of Frost and Konoha enemies!"

"Your lives will prevent that," Kakashi said gently, as his arm ripped into the other man's solar plexus.

"Itachi!" Tenzo.

Itachi caught sight of an enemy coming toward him with a grim look, prepared for death. Holding kunai in both hands, clenching his teeth as he raced toward Itachi, the boy was still not even ten years old.

The Land of Frost was small. Although the larger battles were no more, in a country that still had few ninjas and a national power that was immature, even a child like this had plenty of war potential.

"Gah!" His battle cry already sounded like a sob.

Itachi met the boy head-on. A sharp pain raced through his stomach. The boy's kunai had stabbed him. The slender shoulders shook fiercely as they touched Itachi's belly. The boy's terror had surpassed his limits, and tears began to fill his eyes.

"Itachi!" Kakashi shouted.

"I'm all right," he replied calmly, and Kakashi and the others watched, surrounding him from a distance.

Shaking like a leaf, the boy slowly lifted his face. Tears spilled out of the eyes that looked up at Itachi. "Ah. Aaaunh." His fear became sound, and slipped out of him.

"You're a proper ninja now. Be strong," Itachi told his enemy kindly.

In his confusion and fear, the boy had no idea what was going on. He shook his head from side to side, and desperately tried to turn his eyes away from reality.

"You didn't run away; you came right at me. So, I want to treat you with the courtesy a full-fledged ninja deserves." Itachi grabbed his kunai from behind, so that the boy couldn't see. He ran his blade up from below into the slender nape of his crying enemy's neck. He gently pulled the kunai from his own stomach, and stepped back.

A spray of blood shot out from the boy's neck. None of it splattered Itachi. This, too, was etiquette for a ninja. The young body fell onto the pile of corpses, neither enemy nor ally.

"This is also a battlefield," Itachi murmured, not loud enough for anyone else to hear.

Am I actually getting closer to my dream? Itachi asked himself in his heart. He felt as though his body were gradually growing heavier, buried in the easy flow of time. His childhood days when he prayed with all his heart that he would become a ninja stronger than anyone else were already in the distance, and the bonds coiling about his entire body were trying to trap Itachi in the framework of "just a ninja."

If this is how it is, I want to just walk away from the village, the clan, the Anbu, and be free…

He knew that this would never be allowed.

The boy's eyes, devoid of light, stared endlessly at the troubled Itachi.

∞

"Make a list of the number of expected participants at the time of action, invasion routes, attack targets, and assassination targets. I'd like to decide on the crucial day of action at the next meeting. Put together your opinions before then. If you have any ideas, you can speak them at any time. Simply make sure to be careful of the eyes of the people of the village."

When Fugaku finished speaking, the brethren relaxed for a moment. They were loosening up at the thought of the end of the meeting. But that easy calm was shattered by the tense voice of Yashiro.

"Is Itachi here?"

Itachi felt a disgust at the voice calling his name.

When he didn't answer, the voice called his name again in irritation. "Itachi!"

"I'm here." Itachi raised a heavy arm.

Rather than rebuke Itachi for his attitude, Yashiro simply stared at him with cold eyes. "You were there at the breakdown of negotiations with the Land of Frost the other day, yes?"

Itachi said nothing.

"Answer me."

"Anbu missions are not to be spoken of to outsiders."

"Are you seriously saying that to me?" A deep groove grew between Yashiro's eyebrows.

Itachi stared at the narrow eyes before him without responding.

"For what purpose did you join the Anbu?"

Itachi was silent again.

"To obtain a variety of information from a place close to the center of the village, and report to us," Yashiro answered himself.

"Yashiro." As if to toss his silent son a lifeline, his father said the name of his trusted retainer.

Yashiro made no move to answer him, but simply continued to glare at Itachi. "What have you brought to us since joining the Anbu? Not once have we heard the secrets of the village from your mouth."

"I just don't know any, so I can't talk about them."

"Is it really only that?"

"What is that supposed to mean?" The spirit of rebellion flickered in Itachi's eyes.

Yashiro took this with a daring smile crawling across his face, while a man with long hair stood up beside him. Uchiha Inabi. He, too, was Itachi's father's trusted confidant. "You're turning on us, aren—"

"Enough!" Fugaku roared.

Both Yashiro and Inabi were forced into silence at this rare display of anger from Fugaku. "You both understand exactly what this time means for the clan. We cannot follow through on these serious matters when we are at each other's throats."

The men were silent. Finally, Yashiro sat down; disgruntled, Inabi followed suit.

"You sit, too, Itachi." His father glared. "Itachi."

His father's voice sounded weak to him as he stood there still. Almost like an entreaty.

"Excuse me." The pain in Itachi's chest naturally turned into words, and spilled out.

His father desperately tried to pull everyone together. Why was he being so servile, trying to reconcile everyone? Was the framework of the clan that important? To Itachi, it looked as though his father were being toyed with by the passion of the younger men.

I don't understand...

"At any rate, the next meeting will decide our path. It will be an important meeting. Be aware that absences will not be tolerated."

The meeting ended with turmoil still in the air.

Itachi began to walk home alone, without meeting anyone's eyes. He didn't even see Shisui or Izumi.

2

Danzo looked down at Hiruzen, who was putting his pipe to his lips. They were alone in the Hokage's office.

"Six months since he joined the Anbu, hm?" Hiruzen said, exhaling smoke.

"What are you talking about?"

"Don't play dumb. I'm talking about the boy you have your eyes on."

"Hmph!"

Occasionally, Hiruzen spoke in this sort of roundabout way. "He's carrying out his duties faithfully."

"I see."

"Didn't you come to talk about him?" Hiruzen had seen

through him. For Danzo, who hated more than anyone to have his own thoughts read, it was deeply difficult to endure.

He made a move in return. "It appears you have an Uchiha directly under you now, hm, Hiruzen?"

Hiruzen brought the pipe to his lips, looking at though Danzo had poked a painful spot.

Danzo ignored the look, and continued. "I hear you've removed Uchiha Shisui from his regular duties, and given him permission to move at his own discretion and judgment? And that, in name at least, we have another Uchiha in the Anbu."

"Shisui wanted me to give him the freedom to act. I simply opened the road to him."

"So now the Hokage is listening to the whims of a mere ninja?"

"I simply took into consideration the feelings of someone worried about the Uchiha clan."

"If you give the same consideration to the circumstances of every single person, the village will fall apart."

"I know. I don't need you telling me that!" Hiruzen shouted, revealing his irritation. "How about you stop beating around the bush, and tell me already? What exactly have you come for today, Danzo?"

I should really stop torturing him already, Danzo gloated in his heart, before bringing up the matter he had under consideration.

"Just as you have one of the Uchiha clan under your control, I should like one arranged for me."

Hiruzen made an obviously disgusted face the instant the word "control" left Danzo's mouth. Once he had finished listening, the corners of his mouth turned up slightly as he looked at the other man. "You're saying give Itachi to the Foundation?"

"The thought never even entered my head."

"Don't play dumb."

"I am not playing dumb," Danzo asserted.

Hiruzen narrowed his eyes, measuring Danzo's sincerity. The countless creases around the corners of his eyes deepened. "What are you thinking, then?"

"Why not promote Itachi to team leader?"

"He's still only eleven."

"And Anbu team leaders are to be thirteen or older," Danzo said, a thin smile spreading across his face. "You do have that rule there somewhere, hm?"

Hiruzen got an uncomfortable look on his face. "The Anbu are a division supporting the central pillars of the village. The team leaders who rule over them must have sufficient judgment. Thus, the requirement that they be at least thirteen."

"Sufficient judgment. Itachi already has that."

"That's not the issue."

"Age and the like are meaningless before actual ability." Danzo's firm stance pushed Hiruzen into silence. "Are the rules that important, Hiruzen? The dissatisfaction of the Uchiha clan is already a nearly untenable situation. In order to break through this status quo, we need someone in a position to make effective use of the will of the Foundation, *and* someone connected with you. A mere Anbu ninja won't be able to avoid the orders of his team leader. Promoting Itachi makes it easier for him to move."

"You're saying put him between you and I, without having him belong to the Foundation?"

"That's exactly what I'm saying. No one in the Uchiha clan

can match the abilities of Itachi and Shisui. If we can win those two over, it likely won't be difficult to prevent the explosion of their clan. Just as you gave Shisui special privileges, it is necessary to give a certain amount of the same to Itachi."

"But eleven is simply too young to lead a team." Hiruzen was wavering.

One more little push... "Then, what if he were twelve?"

The third Hokage did not respond.

"Itachi's publicly disclosed age goes up a year, and that neatly takes care of the rule, don't you think?"

"Let me think about it a little more."

"Understood." Danzo was certain. Hiruzen would definitely consent.

∞

"How's school?" Itachi asked his brother as he wet his throat with some cold juice.

"It's way better to train here like this with you." Sasuke smiled, looking up at Itachi from the bench where he sat, clutching in both hands a can with droplets of water forming on it.

"It's way better to train here like this with you." Back when he had first started at the academy, Itachi had said the same sort of thing to Shisui. Once again, he felt keenly how alike he and his brother were.

His mission finished early, so he decided to train with Sasuke once he got home. Because Itachi couldn't spend too much time with him normally, he actively tried to create opportunities. And the time he spent with Sasuke soothed Itachi more than anything else in his life. Sweating together with his little brother, he could escape his everyday troubles.

When did it start being like this?

Lately, whenever he saw Shisui, all they did was talk about where the clan was headed. It had been who knew how many years since they trained together. Even talking with Izumi, his attention ended up focused on her feelings, and he couldn't stay free of obstructive thoughts. He knew he was too involved there, but he couldn't help it. In the end, it was only when he was training with his brother that he could just be himself, without thinking about anything.

"Is school boring?"

"No, it's not, but..." Sasuke mumbled, staring at the opening in his can.

Itachi had a pretty good idea of what his baby brother was thinking. "Is it that your skills and thinking are too different, so things aren't going too well with your friends?"

Because it had been like that for Itachi. He had been able to do everything better than everyone else, so the other students in his class had seemed very much like children. Their way of thinking, and the way they faced things, had been too juvenile; he hadn't been able to talk with them with the same sense of values. He wondered absently if it wasn't the same for Sasuke. He felt like his brother shared the same awkwardness he did when it came to interacting with people.

"I don't especially want it to go well or anything. I mean, those guys, their ninjutsu and their schoolwork are just totally no good."

"What about Naruto?"

"Huh?" Sasuke's eyes widened at the unexpected name that came out of his brother's mouth. The gaze he turned upward to Itachi was clouded with surprise.

Itachi himself was surprised. He didn't know why he had said Naruto's name. The child with the golden hair who was the same age as his little brother had simply popped into his head.

"He's a total disaster, no matter what they make us do. And he's always finding a reason to bug me. He's super annoying."

"So, Naruto bugs you?"

"I don't think about him at all, but then he'll come over to me, and start complaining and stuff."

If his little brother's position at school was no different from Itachi's when he had been there, then Itachi assumed the other students gave Sasuke a wide berth. While they acknowledged his abilities, none of them truly tried to befriend him.

However, Naruto walked right up to Sasuke.

The boy boasting he would be Hokage came back to life in Itachi's mind. That poor child with the Nine Tails in his body; no one wanted anything to do with him. Despite this, he had unshakeable faith in his big dreams. His bearing, his way of talking, everything about him was the polar opposite of Sasuke.

But when Itachi imagined the two of them together, it seemed strangely fitting. "He comes over to you because he's curious about you. Be nice to him."

"I can't be nice to a kid like that."

"It'd be nice if you could someday," Itachi said, placing the palm of his hand on Sasuke's head.

"There's totally no way!" Sasuke shut his eyes tightly, his nose crinkling up, and gritted his teeth.

Unconsciously, Itachi burst out laughing at the funny expression. His little brother relaxed his face, and also started to laugh.

The warm evening passed peacefully.

3

Sitting with his arms crossed and his eyes closed, Fugaku listened to the sound of the sliding door closing, and opened his eyes.

His own room. He was sitting cross-legged, looking at the alcove where the seat of honor was set on his right, his back turned to the wall of the right side of the room. It was his own son opening the sliding door that led to the hall, and showing his face.

"Did you need something, Father?" His too-talented son made no attempt to warm the recent, excessive chill in his voice, as he stayed outside the door.

"Come in," Fugaku urged.

Itachi finally, reluctantly, stepped over the threshold to the room. He closed the sliding door behind him, and sat down properly on his knees before his father.

"I heard you went to the park with Sasuke."

"I did."

He had seen the two come home covered in sweat, and called Itachi in after his bath. His younger son was sitting at the table, and talking with his mother.

"I have to prepare for my mission tomorrow. I'd appreciate it if you could be brief about your business," Itachi said, face stiffening, clearly on guard against his father.

It was no wonder. Recently, they hadn't had any semblance of a conversation. About the only opportunity they had to hear each other's voices was at the regular meetings. And with all eyes on him, Fugaku couldn't put on a fatherly face there. Given that they had nothing but formal contact with each other, like strangers, it was only natural that a distance would grow between them.

"Don't speak so stiffly," Fugaku said, and smiled. It was the best smile he could muster. In general, he rarely smiled. As the head of the Military Police Force, as the man who pulled together all the young people of the clan, he felt that he must not show reckless emotion.

No... When he thought about it, he had never really smiled, not since he was little.

Which reminded him. When had he last seen his son smile? He couldn't remember.

My son and I are alike... A strange joy rose up in his chest.

The delight Fugaku felt at that moment was different from the simple emotion of a parent at their child resembling them. His son was the genius of the academy, passing his chunin exams on his own, the first Uchiha posted to the Anbu. And Fugaku's joy came from the fact that such a storied ninja would resemble him.

It was fairly twisted for a father to see his own son as an object of aspiration. Fugaku himself was very aware of that. Which was why, sometimes, he found his son unpleasant. As a man—rather than as a father—he was forced to acknowledge the fact that he had lost. This led to the cool attitude he adopted toward Itachi. He knew it was foolish as a parent. But his pride as a ninja simply could not rejoice in Itachi's advancement in the world.

And now his son was starting to move away from him.

"How is your work with the Anbu?" he asked, still smiling.

Itachi looked at him with wary eyes. "As long as I am putting into practice the things I've learned since graduating from the academy, there is no *how*."

It was a model answer. Apparently, his dispassionate son had the idea that at that moment, he was interacting with the man who governed the young people of the clan, rather than his father.

"Yashiro and Inabi aren't here," Fugaku remarked, trying hard to keep his tone gentle. "I'm your father, and you are my son. Those are the only people in this room."

Itachi was a clever child. All Fugaku had to say was that, and the boy seemed to understand his father's thinking. Still, Itachi did not immediately become open and straightforward, the way he had when he was five or six. His guard relaxed slightly; that was the extent of his heart softening. Even so, his eyes became much calmer than they had been. "Things haven't changed, really, from when I wasn't in the Anbu."

"You're not doing any difficult work?"

"There is some of that," his son murmured. And then he lowered his eyes for an instant, before looking straight at his father once more. "Given that I'm in the Anbu, no weakness can be tolerated."

"That's my boy." His favorite thing to say. When he was praising his son, those were always the words he used. But at some point, it started feeling like he was saying it to bolster himself, rather than his son. Trying to keep his talented son beneath him, he bound him with the words "my boy." That's what he felt like.

Saying it was already a habit. When he wanted to praise his son, the words came out before he even had the chance to think, so that after he said, "that's my boy," a sharp thorn would stab into his heart. And again that day, Fugaku felt the pain in his chest.

"Don't worry about things at the meeting," he said, as if to push aside the uneasiness in the area of his solar plexus.

"What?" His son looked surprised at his words. He was likely assuming Fugaku would rebuke him for the exchange with Yashiro and the others at the meeting. Itachi was surprised at having that expectation betrayed.

"It's not as though everyone in the clan thinks the same way. I have no intention of forcing our thinking on you. Rather than a stone drifting along with the strong current, I want you to be a man, like a rock that stands against the current, and pierces it."

"Father..."

"You do not need to yield in your own thinking. If you cannot accept what Yashiro and the others say, then you can stand up, and proudly assert your own ideas."

"But it doesn't seem like they would tolerate that at the meeting."

"It is indeed as you say." A sigh slipped from between

Fugaku's lips. "The young people are moved by passion, and they lose sight of themselves. And they expel those who don't agree with them, charging forward toward what they believe to be lofty."

"Father," Itachi murmured.

"What? Say it."

"All right." Looking as though he had resolved himself, the boy began to speak. "Do you have a different opinion than they do, Father?"

"I do not," Fugaku asserted. "My feelings are the same as theirs. I am simply not so young as to cast out differing ideas." His son's disappointment was so clear, he could almost pick it up in his hand.

"Is that so..."

The boulder had already begun to roll. There was nothing to be done about it at this late date. Or rather, Fugaku had no intention of doing anything. Rising to action was the only possibility left to their clan.

But he did not want to force his son to obey. "You should stay true to your thinking. Fight, be confused, be lost, and come through that to find your answer. And once you find it, make your decision, and do not waver from it. Find your answer, and be ready to follow through. That is determination."

"Determination..."

"Yes. There are few people in this world who live their lives with their own determination. They leave their decisions to others, and avert their eyes from responsibility. You must not live like that, at least. Move forward in your life, making your own decisions." Fugaku felt something hot in his eyes. He tried desper-

ately to calm the emotions in his heart without his son noticing.

"I understand," Itachi said, like a small battle cry, and turned passionate eyes on his father. "I will never leave the decisions in my own life to someone else."

"Now *that* is my boy." For the first time in a long time, Fugaku was able to say the words in a straightforward way. There was no pain in his heart.

∞

The slight trembling of Hiruzen's eyebrows did not escape Danzo's notice.

The formal meeting room at the Hokage Residence, the seat where budgetary policy for the governance of the village of Konohagakure was determined. In addition to Hiruzen and Danzo, the councilors Koharu and Homura were there. At this meeting, they would set the basic policy, and, taking that into consideration, Hiruzen would select the personnel in village government and the official budgets.

"About the budget for the Military Police Force." Taking his eyes off the document he had before him, Hiruzen looked at the other three. In his hand was their proposal. "The basic idea *is* to significantly reduce the budget, but what exactly is the meaning of this, Koharu?"

Hearing her name, Utatane Koharu opened her eyes a narrow slit and peered at Hiruzen. "It's been seven years since the end of the war. Life has gotten back to normal, for the most part. And it has become customary for the Anbu to investigate serious and brutal crimes. The current role of the Military Police Force is quite limited. There's no need for the same budget they've had in the past, is there?"

"That said, isn't cutting their budget by forty percent a bit too abrupt? A cut like this will also have a significant effect on Military Police Force personnel."

Staring at the sour look on Hiruzen's face, Mitokado Homura opened his mouth. "Rebuilding after the Nine Tails' attack is mostly complete. The urgent need now is for new facilities and wider roads. And now that early graduation has been abolished, the academy will need to expand soon, as well. We don't have the extra resources for a shrinking organization."

"I know. I know that, but if we do this in such a way that we make the Military Police Force alone the enemy, it will be increasingly—"

"It will spur dissatisfaction among them?" Danzo spat, seizing his opportunity. He continued without a pause. "I will ask you then, is there another division in this village that is growing smaller as obviously as the Military Police Force? The cause for the reduction is clear: peace in the village, and the expansion of Anbu duties. The Military Police Force can perform no other role than maintaining the peace. And given the negative feelings of dissatisfaction they harbor toward the village, it's doubtful as to whether or not they are faithfully performing even that role. I feel that maintaining their current budget is simply pampering them."

"It is not pampering. It's sheltering."

"Sheltering? Why would people with no impediment to their work need to be sheltered?"

"Because the places where they can be active have been se-

verely limited by people like you, who are prejudiced against that clan!" Hiruzen pounded his desk and stood up, as Homura and Koharu watched coolly.

Rather than pushing back the grin that spread across his face, Danzo turned to the third Hokage, his old acquaintance, and said, "So, you would shelter them because there is prejudice. Isn't that in and of itself an act of distancing and discrimination?"

"What did you—"

"It's precisely because they have the Military Police Force to work at, and because they are assured a more than ample budget from the village, that the Uchiha clan refuse contact with outsiders, and sneak around with people from their own circle. You distance them in the framework of the Military Police Force under the pretext of sheltering them, and so you allow them to grow this evil flower of dissatisfaction within themselves. Isn't that so?"

"The formation and management of the Military Police Force was the dying wish of the second Hokage."

"Don't you feel that way of thinking is outdated?" Danzo asked. "I believe a revolution is necessary, now especially when the Great War is over, and the scars from Nine Tails' attack are beginning to heal. But, what does everyone else think?"

"I have no objection," Koharu voiced her agreement. Homura nodded silently. Danzo had already gone round to speak to them, and the three were of the same opinion on the matter of reducing the Military Police Force budget.

Only Hiruzen was on the outside. "And what will we do when the Uchiha clan's dissatisfaction explodes?"

"You're using Shisui to prevent that, are you not?" Danzo

struck the final blow.

It hit home. Hiruzen faltered.

"Wasn't that the reason you pulled the young ninja, so worried about his clan, from his regular missions, gave him a position in name only, and permitted him a certain level of independence?"

"Thirty percent, then," Hiruzen said hoarsely.

A bitter choice.

He was acting exactly as Danzo had expected. Danzo didn't believe a reduction of forty percent was possible, either. He had anticipated thirty percent being the point of compromise.

"If we cut any more than thirty percent of their budget, we won't escape backlash from the Military Police Force."

"I respect the Hokage's decision."

Hiruzen made an obviously disgusted face at Danzo's seemingly deliberate words.

4

Shisui had called him to their usual cliff.

It was already the middle of the night. The village and the compound were asleep. Still, the eyes of the Anbu who watched over the compound were open.

During Itachi's work monitoring the clan, he had memorized the angles of all the cameras watching them. He had already devised a route that allowed him to move freely through the compound, slipping through the slight gaps that rose up in

the angles between cameras. He had only told Shisui about the Anbu's monitoring, and the route through their blind spots.

Shisui was the sole ninja he could trust. He definitely wouldn't leak the information to anyone else. He should have been making his way to the cliff through the blind spot route as well.

No one knew about their meeting.

Once Itachi had slipped through the compound and escaped the eyes of the cameras, he ran. The moon, in its last quarter, glittered nearby in the center of the sky. Beneath shining stars that looked as though they would come tumbling down, he ran intently, keeping to the shadows.

The forest abruptly split, revealing his destination, the cliff, a human figure on the edge of the rough rock. Standing with his back to Itachi, Shisui was staring at the raging river that could be seen below the cliff.

Itachi raced over, and stopped behind him. "Sorry to make you wait."

"I just got here, too," Shisui said, turning around, exhaustion obvious on his face. He had faint bags under his eyes, and his cheeks were a little hollow. His jaw, significantly tapered down, looked more like a mark of overwork than growth into adulthood.

"You look really tired."

"Things have been happening." Shisui dropped his eyes, a shadow he couldn't hide clinging to his face.

"I know I said we'd work together," Itachi said in a gentle voice, as if sympathizing with his friend. "Sorry for always leaving things to you."

"You can't do anything that would cause you to neglect your missions. We're both in the Anbu, but I've got permission from the Lord Hokage to move freely. It's only natural I'd be working. There's nothing for you to feel bad about."

His friend was kind enough to say that, but Itachi keenly felt his own worthlessness. Even as they shared the same determination to prevent their clan's coup d'état, what exactly had he done? Shisui had gotten the right to act alone to dig into the clan's conspiracy, and was investigating their movements day and night. Unlike him. Itachi was always putting the clan off, swamped with his daily missions.

Even still, Shisui treated Itachi as someone of the same mind. Which was exactly why they had slipped away from the eyes of their monitors to meet outside the compound like this.

"Before I get into it, there's something I want to tell you," Shisui started, his gaze so sharp, it was painful. "The clan suspects you."

"You don't have to tell me that. I know."

"A ninja of the clan's been ordered to monitor you."

"What?" The clan was watching Itachi. And Shisui was saying that the one accepting this role was a ninja of the same clan. Who in the clan was in a position to hand down orders to his brethren...?

His father.

"I can't believe he would—"

"It's true, Itachi. I witnessed it myself, so there's no doubt about it."

"What do you mean?"

"I mean, the one given the task of watching you is me."

Shisui's words pierced his heart. His father had ordered Shisui to watch him?

"They're using the fact that I'm close to you. Three senior officials from the Military Police Force came to order me to monitor you," Shisui said, as if hearing Itachi's voice in his head.

Three senior officials...

"Yashiro, Inabi, Tekka. They suspect you. And you and Yashiro did have some fierce words at the meeting." Shisui was covertly telling him that it wasn't his father.

But his father was in the position to give orders to those three. Even if Yashiro and the others were the ones who approached Shisui, Itachi didn't know exactly where that order had originated. A black doubt rose up in his heart, the polar opposite of the love he had felt at his father's kind words earlier. Exactly which one was his real father?

"I probably don't need to say this, but I'll make some things up, and report back to them. So you can relax."

He didn't doubt Shisui.

"But there's no doubt that the radicals in the clan have their eyes on you."

"I was ready for that."

"That firmness is both a good thing and a weak point for you, you know," Shisui said, smiling. "I like it." His friend turned his eyes up to the sky, and took in the moon hanging in the dark.

"You have this strength, like no matter what happens to you, your way of thinking will never be shaken. If it's to do what you believe in, you'll stand and face whatever enormous force might rise up before you without flinching. Which is exactly why I can trust you. And..." Shisui turned his eyes away from the slice of moon, and slid his eyes along the ground before looking directly at Itachi. "I can tell you what I've decided."

"What happened, Shisui?"

"You know what day tomorrow is, right?"

Itachi nodded silently. The regular meeting of the clan.

Last time, his father had said that this meeting would be critical: they would decide the schedule for the coup. In other words, at the meeting the following day, the consensus of opinion of the clan would be confirmed, and the resolve to act would become fixed.

"If everything goes as usual at the meeting tomorrow, we won't be able to stop things."

"What are you planning to do?"

"Tomorrow, I'm going to attack your father on his way to Nakano Shrine."

Itachi couldn't stop his heart from racing.

"Relax. I'm not going to kill Lord Fugaku or anything. I'm just going to trap him in a genjutsu."

"The sharingan you used that time with Mukai?"

"Exactly." Shisui's eyes glowed red in the darkness. And then, the three magatama patterns in each eye grew larger, and merged into one. "Mangekyo sharingan."

After that day, Itachi had looked into this himself. In old Uchiha documents, only the existence of the Mangekyo sharingan was noted; the record stopped with the mention that its power far surpassed that of the normal sharingan. It further noted that the number of people who had activated this sharingan could be counted on both hands, perhaps, and that even for members of the clan, it was a visual jutsu with many unknowns.

"Even Lord Fugaku, the fearsome 'Wicked Eye,' won't be able to avoid these eyes."

"But I mean, trapping him in a genjutsu, what are you actually going to do?"

"At the same time as I awakened these eyes, I got a certain jutsu. A jutsu called 'Kotoamatsukami.'"

"Kotoamatsukami." Itachi felt an indescribable unearthliness in the word.

"It puts the person trapped in the genjutsu into a state of total unawareness; then, you can make them do what you want."

Itachi understood that this was basically what visual jutsu was; whether or not the target was aware of what was happening was determined by the ninja applying the jutsu. The ninja incited an awareness in the target that they were caught in a jutsu, leading the target to doubt everything, and get caught up in the jutsu. Or else the target unconsciously sank bit by bit into the jutsu, so that by the time they realized what was going on, there was nothing they could do about it. This Kotoamatsukami fell into the latter category, which wasn't particularly uncommon for a visual jutsu.

"The advantage of this technique is that the effect and the duration are both multiplied because of the power of the Mangekyo sharingan," Shisui added.

As if urging him to explain, Itachi stayed silent, and continued to stare at his friend's strange sharingan.

"For the visual jutsu of a normal sharingan, your gaze has to intersect with the gaze of your intended target to some degree. You need that direct action, and the flow of chakra. But the Mangekyo sharingan allows me to sidestep all that a bit. I just have to look at my target's eyes, and I can pour my chakra in, even if our gazes aren't intersecting. And the amount of chakra is several times more than with normal sharingan. So the target falls into the visual jutsu instantly. They have no idea anything's even happened."

"So you mean by the time the enemy sees you, they're already in the jutsu?"

"That's it exactly."

"And you're going to use that on my father?"

Shisui nodded forcefully. "If I can just get him in Kotoamatsukami, I can make Lord Fugaku tell everyone the coup is off. And I can make Fugaku himself believe from the bottom of his heart that it was his own idea."

"You can write over the mind of the ringleader?"

"It's only the fact that it's your father that makes me hesitate."

"You don't have to worry about that," Itachi asserted. If it were to stop a coup d'état, he would gladly do anything, even if it meant reaching into his own father's mind. It was just that the one who could actually execute this plan was Shisui.

"Don't come to the meeting tomorrow, Itachi."

"Why not?"

"The radical faction suspects you. If I make Lord Fugaku's attitude change abruptly, you're the first one they'll point their fingers at. I don't know what they'll do if you're at the meeting."

"You're saying they'd attack me?" Itachi thought that would be just fine. The few years since he became a ninja had taught him that in order to avoid a large fight, sometimes, you couldn't avoid a small one. To rid this world of all fighting, a serious sac-

rifice was necessary. "If they attack me, I'll just fight them off."

"Yashiro and the rest don't have a chance against you. But that skirmish would inevitably interrupt this important meeting."

"So you're going to take control of my father, and force everyone to go in the other direction, huh?"

"Yeah." Shisui grabbed Itachi's shoulders. "If I pull it off, the clan's enthusiasm for the coup should drop. We knock down Lord Fugaku, create an opening, and gradually win members of the clan over to the anti-war side."

"Isn't there anything I can do?"

"Wait here until the meeting's over."

"But—"

"It'll definitely work." Shisui grinned forcefully. "I'll come here to report the results of the meeting. Just wait 'til then. The next time we meet, the clan will have taken a step toward peace. We'll need your strength after that. I know you'll be critical, given how far beyond the clan you've gone. So you totally can't die before then, no matter what happens. Leave everything to me tomorrow. Please." His good friend bowed his head deeply.

"Sorry I can't help at such an important time as this," Itachi said, lowering his own head.

"Itachi." His friend tightened his grip on his shoulders. "Our fight starts tomorrow."

"I've been ready for a long time."

5

"What? You know just what tomorrow means!!" In the dead of night, his father's roar echoed throughout the house.

Itachi's first reaction was not fear of his father, or concern about his rage. It was the trivial thought, *Did that yell wake Sasuke up?*

His little brother had school in the morning. Knowing nothing of the ominous shadow that hung over the entire clan, Sasuke spent his days concentrating on himself and his own work. His little brother needed his precious sleep to recharge his batteries for the following day, and Itachi didn't want it interrupted by a boorish roar of anger.

His father's room. His parents were both sitting in front of him. His father had his arms crossed, and was glaring at his son, while beside him, his mother's eyebrows were raised, and her mouth turned downward at the corners. Seeing this, Itachi realized for the first time that his mother and his father felt the same way.

He had never once spoken with his mother about the clan issues or the meetings. His mother didn't ask, and he hadn't initiated any such conversation. Because she had never once spoken about these matters with his father while he was present, he hadn't known before now just how she viewed the clan. But in that instant, he understood everything.

His mother, sitting next to his father and his obvious anger, was a member of the clan, and in favor of the coup. When he thought about it, it was only natural. She was not the sort of

wife to shout out objections when her own husband was the leader of the scheme. Even just reasoning from her gentle temperament, he saw that she was not the sort of person who would go against his father's wishes.

Itachi had known this about her. But even knowing it, he was still quite shocked to see her feelings on display before him like this. Itachi faced his father, trying not to look at his mother to the extent possible.

An aura flickered on the other side of the sliding door behind him.

Sasuke...

So his father's loud voice earlier *had* woken him up. A flame of anger sprang to life in Itachi's heart. His father completely lacked consideration for his little brother.

Fugaku had forgotten about Sasuke the day before the entrance ceremony, and tried to go along on Itachi's mission, and now, this angry roar. Even when he looked at his brother's report cards—always straight As—he didn't really say anything to the boy. His mother had told Itachi that Sasuke was disappointed by this, and he couldn't help but feel so sorry for his little brother.

Recently, Sasuke's feelings toward his big brother had become more complicated. He had gotten the mistaken idea that their father only ever looked at Itachi, and a faint jealousy had taken root in his heart.

Itachi wanted to shout at Sasuke that he had it all wrong. Their father didn't see Itachi as his son; he saw Itachi as a useful tool, necessary for his own ambitions to carry out a coup d'état. Itachi's relationship with their father was definitely not what his little brother thought it was.

What was Itachi actually getting yelled at for in that moment? Not for going against his father's wishes as a son, or for acting incorrectly as a human being. No, his father was furious that Itachi would not be at the meeting that was so critical to his own aspirations.

Itachi steeled himself and opened his mouth, as if to brush aside his father's hatred. "I have a mission tomorrow."

"What mission?!"

The foolish question exhausted Itachi. At the very least, his father knew that Itachi was obligated to keep Anbu missions confidential. He couldn't simply answer just because he was asked.

"I can't say. It's top secret," he replied, his irritation growing. The naive questioning was an obvious annoyance, but he was also frustrated by the fact that his parents were so absorbed in the conversation that they didn't even notice his brother's aura.

Hearing the words "top secret," his father closed his eyes, arms still crossed. His always tightly closed lips were pressed even more firmly together, and he stayed silent, tension oozing from every pore on his body. His mother turned worried eyes on her husband. Both of their faces shone with a thin layer of sweat.

A silence that was difficult to endure filled the room. Worried that Sasuke might not be able to withstand this tense atmosphere, and collapse, Itachi focused his mind on the aura behind him.

"Itachi," his father said, and then paused before speaking again. "You are a pipeline that connects the clan with the center of the village." His eyes were colored a faint red, but they didn't

change so much that the pattern of the sharingan rose up in them.

A pipeline connecting the clan and the center of the village...

A spy, basically. *You push this dirty job on your own son, and now you have to pester him about it?* Itachi asked his father, silently. Naturally, he did not get an answer; his father's sharp gaze simply hurt, and stabbed through his tattered heart.

"You...know that, yes?"

"Mm hmm." It was all he could do to offer that answer.

If he were to do exactly as his father wished, and work in a way that would delight Yashiro and the younger people of the clan, what on earth would become of the village? The 24-hour monitoring of the clan by the Anbu. Danzo's request to provide information about the clan. These bits alone were more than enough to enrage his father and the others. The plan to stage a coup, already advanced to the stage where they were about to decide on a specific day, would be accelerated, and the resentment of the young people toward the village would reach its peak. And what would come after that?

War.

And then the defeat of the Uchiha clan, and persecution greater than anything they had seen before.

Itachi had come to understand only too well in his life as a ninja that the village of Konohagakure was most certainly not pure and innocent. It wasn't just a prejudice toward the Uchiha clan. They had sealed the Nine Tails in a newborn baby, and then, with only the baby himself unaware of this fact, they had isolated him, surrounding him at a distance. The Anbu was the same. The Hokage himself had organized this institution that bore the burden of the darkness of the village, and singlehand-edly forced them to take on dark work behind the scenes.

This village took the things it didn't want to look at, foisted them on someone else, and then pretended not to see. In a place like this, would the clan be able to live as it had after being de-feated in an attempted coup?

No. The path his father was attempting to walk was a road to ruin.

Itachi's thoughts were shattered by his father's voice.

"Bear this in mind."

What did "this" indicate? Floating in a sea of thought, Itachi had for an instant lost sight of what Fugaku was talking about. And then, he remembered that his father was referring to the "pipeline connecting the clan with the center of the village."

"And you will come to the meeting tomorrow," his father continued.

Itachi stayed silent. He could not go. He had promised Shisui.

Still, he couldn't muster the energy to declare here and now that he would not go. If he did, his father would get even more enraged. And if that happened, this conversation would go on even longer. He couldn't sit here with his father any longer.

Sorry, Sasuke, he apologized to his brother in his heart, be-fore turning his eyes away from his father, and toward the aura behind him.

"Sasuke. If you're done in the washroom, hurry up and go to back to bed."

In that moment, his mother and father appeared to notice his younger brother's presence for the first time. The sliding door

behind Itachi slowly opened, and Sasuke stuck his head in apologetically.

"A-all right."

His father stood up, and looked at Sasuke. His eyes had already stopped seeing Itachi. "What are you doing wandering around in the middle of the night? Hurry up, and go to bed!" Fugaku called, in a voice that was very close to a reprimand.

The anger bleeding into his father's words wasn't purely toward his brother for being up so late. His anger at having an important discussion interrupted won out. Actually, that was all it was.

Perhaps cleverly understanding their father's mental state, Sasuke simply answered, sadly, "All right." He lifted his hanging head, and turned toward Itachi.

His eyes are blaming me for something...

What on earth could his brother be blaming him for? Because he had revealed Sasuke's presence there? Or because the boy thought it was Itachi who had put their father in such a state? Or simply because he was jealous of his older brother having their mother and father all to himself?

In Sasuke's eyes, brimming with emotion, there was a depth that didn't allow Itachi to read the younger boy's true intentions. He was spurred by the urge to know what his brother was thinking, even if he had had to use the sharingan, but he didn't actually do anything.

There was only one thing in Itachi's heart. A desire to atone for having used his little brother to cut short the conversation with their father.

6

Danzo looked at the boy standing in front of him, and thought there was not enough darkness in him. Not compared with another ninja of the same clan, Itachi.

"I hear there is a meeting at Nakano Shrine tomorrow?"

"Given that you live in the darkness of the village, it's no surprise you would know that. But even with that in mind, I have to admit part of me is dumbfounded that even this clan secret is known."

"It is a reality of this village."

"So you're saying you were just letting us go for the time being?"

"You are indeed wise, Uchiha Shisui." Danzo said the name of the ninja standing before him. "I have a question for such a wise ninja."

"I don't have a lot of time, so keep it short."

"Yes, it would be unpleasant if you missed your chance to attack Fugaku, after all."

A crease cut across the space between Shisui's brows. "Even that..."

"Don't get the wrong idea. I did not hear it from Hiruzen's mouth. And it goes without saying Itachi did not leak it. One of my men looked into it."

A line of sweat rolled down the forehead of the wise youth.

"I can't say that controlling Fugaku with your visual jutsu and bringing the plan for a coup d'état to a halt is a particularly good idea." Danzo put a hand to his chin as he stared at the

young ninja. "The majority of the clan is already leaning toward the coup. Flipping the ringleader Fugaku at this stage, you're just spitting into the ocean."

"I won't know unless I tr—"

"I have made it through two great wars, and I am telling you, your plan will most certainly fail." Danzo's severity closed Shisui's mouth. "Even if you succeed in controlling Fugaku with visual jutsu, proposing a halt to action at the meeting today, and managing to pull off this stopgap, nothing will change. The radical faction will only think Fugaku's change of heart is because he has become cowardly in his old age. They will quickly pick a new leader, and move to put the plan into action. Listen to me, Shisui." He put his will into his left eye, and shot a look at the wide-eyed younger man. "The head can always be replaced."

"Don't talk like it's all done already!" Shisui's simple rage looked to Danzo like nothing more than a tantrum.

"That Mangekyo sharingan. I would be able to use it more effectively."

"Wha—" Shisui tried to jump back, and get some distance between them.

But.

In that moment, he realized that he couldn't move his legs.

"Insects are such interesting creatures," Danzo said, taking a step forward. "When a human being is bitten by a mosquito, the pain is nothing. Not even the sensation of being bitten, once the itching is gone." He took another step closer to Shisui. "But the poison of a scorpion, or a spider, can bring even an enormous beast to death at times."

"Wh-what did you do?"

Without responding, Danzo took another step. "If there were an insect which bit like a mosquito, but had the poison of a scorpion in its bite, it would be irresistible."

Abruptly, the world behind Shisui shimmered, and a man appeared. He was wearing a white tiger mask.

Trembling, Shisui turned his face slowly, and looked at the man over his shoulder. Ignoring this, Danzo directed his words toward Tiger Mask.

"What are you calling yourself now?"

"I GO BY SUGARU."

"Oh, that's right." A few more decisive steps, and Danzo was within arm's reach of Shisui. "This man is from the Aburame clan. Given how wise you are, now that I've told you that, you need no further explanation, hm?"

"Ngh!" Shisui gritted his teeth, trying to move somehow. His strong figure was so pitiable, Danzo's lips naturally twisted into the form of a smile.

"Relax. It is not a poison that will kill you right away. You will live just long enough for both of your eyes to be plucked out." Danzo was already close enough that all he had to do was lift up his hand, and he would be touching Shisui's face. "They're fresher plucked out while you're still alive, and they adapt faster, too."

"Danzo... What are you..."

"I'm doing this," Danzo said, as he reached out his left hand.

His index and middle fingers reached up, along with his thumb, and touched Shisui's right eye. He pushed back the upper eyelid with his index and middle fingers, and the lower one with his thumb, gradually revealing the slick, shining eyeball.

ITACHI'S STORY
[MIDNIGHT]

Without a moment's hesitation, he stabbed his fingers into the eye socket. He felt the warmth of the orb on the palm of his hand.

I finally have the Mangekyo sharingan. Delight danced in Danzo's heart.

"And one more," he murmured. And then, he had no sooner wondered if Shisui's remaining eye was shining faintly, than it suddenly disappeared from before him.

"BODY FLICKER," Sugaru muttered.

"Hurry! After him!" Danzo roared, and Sugaru leapt into action. The auras of his subordinates on standby around them also disappeared. "We cannot allow him to live."

In the end, it was Itachi who would realize Danzo's long-held ambition. Shisui was nothing more than an obstacle. If he hadn't had the Mangekyo sharingan, an item beyond his station, Danzo wouldn't have bothered to get directly involved.

"Kill him. Make sure you kill him." Danzo's voice could not reach the subordinates disappearing into the darkness. But even so, he couldn't help but give the order.

∞

Regardless of the outcome, Shisui would come here.

Standing on the cliff as promised, Itachi waited alone for the arrival of his friend. The sun had started to sink to the west, and night would press in on him there soon enough. Only a little longer before the meeting started. Most likely, right around that time, Shisui was controlling his father's thoughts with the power of the Mangekyo sharingan. The meeting would be at least two hours, even if it ran short. He had time. And during that time, Itachi intended to think about what they were going to do from then on.

While they did share the desire to prevent a coup d'état by the clan for the sake of peace in the village, Itachi had always left concrete action to his friend. Shisui had gotten permission from the third Hokage, investigated the movements of the clan on his own, and thought up the current plan. All of it had been Shisui's work. Itachi had done nothing.

Shisui had said the real fight would start after Fugaku was turned against the coup. And it was unlikely that the hot-blooded younger members of the clan would abruptly turn around just because of his father's change of heart. The result of Shisui's action that night would probably be some hesitation, and the postponement of the time for action. But the radicals would regroup and find another path; they would have their coup.

What could they do once they brought his father down? *This* was the most important thing if they were going to realize their shared ambition. Itachi couldn't leave everything to Shisui anymore. He had to think long and hard himself. And then, for the first time, he might be on equal footing with Shisui at last.

"Ngh!" Sensing an aura behind him, Itachi whirled around. "Shisui?" he said, stunned. It was too early for his friend to be there.

"Sorry, Itachi." Blood had spilled down from the closed lids of Shisui's right eye, and dried on his cheek. He walked past Itachi on unsteady feet to stand on the edge of the cliff.

It was obvious that something bad had happened, and his

friend had come to tell him. Itachi simply stayed silent, and waited.

"I failed."

"What happened to your eye?"

Shisui didn't answer, but stared out beyond the cliff, silently.

Itachi calmed his impatient heart, desperate to hear his friend's story.

"I couldn't even make contact with Lord Fugaku," Shisui said, finally. "The meeting's probably starting right about now. They'll probably decide on the key parts of the coup at the meeting today. Our plan failed."

"That doesn't mean it's over." *My friend's spirit is broken…* "Who got you?"

"Danzo."

Itachi's heart began to pound fiercely. In the back of his mind, the face of that treacherous man sprang to life.

"One of his subordinates uses insects, right?" Shisui said.

"Was he wearing a white tiger mask?"

"He dosed me with a poison. There's no saving me."

Sugaru. He was an Aburame. They used insects.

"Itachi." Shisui's voice was shockingly weak. His friend looked small standing before him, smaller than he had at any other time. Shisui had always run on ahead of Itachi, he had fought alongside him for the sake of the clan, he was basically his older brother, and now the air of death coiled and clung to his back. "It…doesn't look like there's any way now to stop the Uchiha coup. If Konohagakure starts fighting itself, other countries will definitely attack…it'll be war."

*It doesn't look like there's any way to stop the coup…*Those were words he did not want to hear from Shisui's mouth. Had his friend given up on everything? Did death make a person that weak and brittle? Itachi, still tied to the realm of life, couldn't begin to understand what was going on inside Shisui.

"Just when I was about to use Kotoamatsukami, and stop the coup," Shisui said, looking over his shoulder at Itachi, "Danzo stole my right eye. He doesn't trust me. He intends to protect the village in his own way, regardless of how it looks."

Having watched Danzo for many years, Itachi understood. That man trusted no one. Even his old comrade-at-arms, the third Hokage, was suspect somehow.

He protects the village in his own way...Itachi felt a chill run up his spine.

"He probably would've taken my left eye too." Shisui moved his hand toward his still-intact eye. He slipped his fingers into the lids, and tightened his grip. "Before he does, I'm giving it to you." When he pulled his hand away again, the lids of his left eye were closed, fresh blood streaming from between them.

Shisui's eyes were Mangekyo sharingan. If he was entrusting this eye to Itachi, it meant that he was giving him permission to use the power lodged in it. The faith his friend had in him made Itachi's heart hurt.

Shisui...he tried to say, but nothing came out. If he gave voice to his friend's name, he felt like the tears brimming in his own eyes would spill out. He could not cry in front of another person. Even more so when it was his friend, talking to him like this, prepared for death.

"You're my best friend. You're the only one I can ask. This village...the Uchiha name...protect them."

Face turned to his outthrust palm, Shisui kneaded his chakra.

A single bird danced down from empty space, and stopped on his hand. The eye resting in his open palm floated up, covered the bird's left eye, and merged with it, as if sucked in. Although he could no longer see now that he had lost both eyes, Shisui knew that he had entrusted his eye to his friend, and a smile of relief rose up on his face. Without a glance at him, the bird nodded its head, before flying up into a sky dyed with darkness.

"There's one more thing I want to give you." Shisui turned his back to Itachi once more. "But before that, there's something I want you to know."

"What?" It was all Itachi could do to get the word out. The words he really wanted to say would not come out: *"Don't die. Don't give up."*

His friend was prepared to die; these were nothing more than words of convenience. It was pointless to say them. So he didn't. Even still, Itachi screamed in the depths of his heart.

You can't die. If you give up, it's all over. A ninja fights until the end of the end. It's not over yet.

But Itachi's cries couldn't reach his friend.

"I killed my good friend with this hand."

Good friend? Who is he talking about?

At the sudden confession, Itachi's thoughts stopped completely.

"It was a little before I met you," Shisui continued, his voice flat, as if leaving his friend behind.

Itachi couldn't see the look on his face.

"I met a boy at the academy I could call a friend. He fought alongside me after I became a genin too, on the same team. Back then, he was my best friend—we really trusted each other. But..."

Shisui fell silent for a moment. "That didn't last for even a year."

The shocking confession continued further.

"This was right after the war ended. Missions were way harsher than they are now. We were in the middle of a mission with a few other teams to clean up after the war, and we ended up by ourselves in another land. Our luck was bad. We ran into more enemies than we could handle. We were staring right at death."

This tale was from before Itachi became a ninja.

"Fortunately, some of the comrades we got separated from found us. They saved me, but my friend was slow to run. If I had just reached out to him, he wouldn't have had to die."

From what Shisui was saying, he had been quite close by when his friend was killed. The difference between life and death was determined by a slight difference in luck, and that bit of luck had divided the two boys. It definitely hadn't been his fault. But Shisui regretted his friend's death as if it were a crime he had committed.

"It wasn't your fault."

"No." Shisui said, as if to cut Itachi off. "I envied that friend. He was blessed with more talent than me. I was jealous of him, always running out in front of me. So that time, I could have reached out my hand. But I deliberately didn't...I killed him."

Itachi had never realized darkness like this slept in Shisui's heart. He was his best friend. What had he been seeing up to that point? He felt dizzy.

"For several months, I was completely destroyed by the fact that I killed him. It was then. When I met you."

Itachi remembered it clearly. He had been training alone

in preparation for his entry into the academy, when Shisui had suddenly appeared. It had been Shisui who asked if they could be friends.

"I watched you, so intently motivated in your training every day, and I just called out to you without thinking. You were always so forward-looking, always running ahead, and spending time with you helped me pick myself up again, bit by bit. I'm really grateful to you."

I'm the one who's grateful...

Of course, the words didn't come out.

"My friend's death gave me a new power. That was the Mangekyo sharingan."

For the *n*th time, the unexpected blow made Itachi dizzy. Paying no heed to his reeling, Shisui continued.

"Mangekyo sharingan are called up by a power that comes from a fierce emotional blow. Mine were probably awakened by my regret over killing my friend."

"Regret over killing your friend..."

"Right."

Itachi had a bad feeling.

"Kill me, Itachi. Then you'll get the Mangekyo sharingan. And then you'll get even stronger."

"That's—"

"I'm dead either way. So then, it's better if I die after leaving you that power."

Itachi felt something hot in his eyes. In his jumbled mind, he couldn't calmly assess whether it was tears, or the rush of energy presaging the activation of some new power.

"All right—do it, Itachi!"

The words of an older brother to push his little brother forward...
Almost staggering, Itachi took a step forward.

"That's it."

Something lukewarm, like blood, dampened Itachi's cheeks. *Tears...* Stifling his sobs so that Shisui wouldn't notice, he continued to move forward.

"With your abilities, something like the clan can't contain you. I mean, knowing you, you'll even be able to surpass the destiny of the clan. No..."

"Shisui..."

"I think your abilities could even swallow up the ninja worldview."

"My abilities?" Only once he heard his voice did Itachi understand that it was trembling. It was the first time he had heard himself weak like this.

"I'm glad I met you."

Itachi reached trembling arms out toward the back of his best friend.

"I'm counting on you to handle the rest."

Those were his friend's last words.

Darkness...

A pitch-black night without moon or stars. The ebony clouds blanketing the heavens threatened to weep at any moment.

I killed my friend...

His hands on the ground where Shisui had stood, Itachi was slumped over, motionless. His exhausted body was heavy as lead; his tattered, wounded heart refused to pick up the thread of his thoughts. Tears fell one after another from his eyes, and even the

dry feeling in his soul could not stop them. Everything was numb.

No...

Somewhere in his body, now one with the darkness, something smoldered. On dead earth covered in a layer of ice, small sparks crackled and burned. As if seeking out that faint warmth, Itachi dove into his own heart.

There. Two sparks. One in each eye.

In his wounded, exhausted heart, he held them.

Fwoosh.

In the blink of an eye, the sparks became massive flames, and enveloped his entire body. His eyes, the core of the blaze, were hot like magma.

"I did get it, Shisui." A brilliant crimson light shone in his still-weeping eyes. "I promise you. I will stop the clan."

Itachi let the voice of his heart ride on the darkness, with a prayer that it would reach the land of the dead.

6

Golden hawk, clad in the robes

of darkness, singing in

the moonlit night

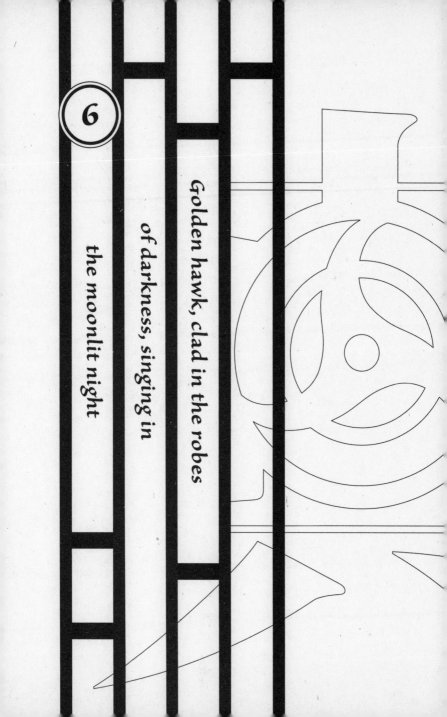

CHAPTER 6

Golden hawk, clad in the robes of darkness, singing in the moonlit night

1

Results beyond reproach. Physical jutsu, ninjutsu, individual, team, battle technique: Sasuke was top of his class in all five subjects. If the early graduation system had still been in place, he would no doubt have been a candidate.

Sitting on the veranda, Itachi closed his little brother's report card, and looked out at the garden. The Uchiha clan crest was proudly drawn on the wall fencing off the grounds. Sasuke stared at it, sad somehow.

"'Keep this up, and you'll be just as amazing as your older brother,' he said." Sasuke muttered their father's words dully. His negativity toward their father bled into his lifeless tone.

No...

Those feelings were toward Itachi.

Sasuke had simply wanted their father to recognize his achievements. But rather than understanding this, Fugaku had compared him with Itachi. For the child Sasuke, "like your older brother," no matter how well intentioned, could never be praise. He was at an age where more than anything, he wanted to be

115

noticed. How upset was he with his big brother? Not having an older brother himself, Itachi couldn't truly understand how Sasuke felt.

Which was why he had decided to simply ask him.

"Are you upset with me?" he asked, a smile rising up on his face as he looked up at the evening sky, visible above the square wall.

Sasuke's eyes grew wide in surprise, as though Itachi had read his mind. His reply was apparently wordless. He silently turned an upset gaze toward his brother.

"That's fine," Itachi started, gently. "I mean, it is true ninjas live hated by other people."

Itachi himself didn't remember how many he had killed. Those countless dead had had families and friends. For those people, he was a loathsome foe they would always hate. *What happened to Kohinata Mukai's sick child*? he wondered suddenly.

"I-I don't think..." His little brother faltered again. Sasuke was upset with his brother, but that wasn't all of it. Sasuke's honest and innocent eyes told Itachi there was also a love that won out over the bad feelings.

My own abilities torment my brother...

After all, Sasuke was plenty talented himself. He certainly wouldn't get stuck looking backward. Even so, the enormity of Itachi's existence threatened to crush him.

"Ha, ha. It's tough being the best." He smiled as well as he could, and looked at his younger brother. "Having power means being isolated, and it leads to arrogance. No matter how high people's hopes were for you."

The Uchiha clan wanted Itachi's genius. But when he didn't

do what they wanted, they were annoyed, until finally, they ordered Shisui to watch him. If he had been a little more ingratiating, perhaps he could have built a friendlier relationship. It was Itachi's own vision that would not allow that.

Rid this world of fighting...

A dream everyone had, that no one actually took seriously. But Itachi would not allow any compromises on the road to realizing this dream of his, because it was such a grand dream that if he permitted himself even a tiny compromise, he would never be able to make it come true. Which was why he couldn't go along with them.

And as a result, Shisui...

Sasuke looked at his brother with worried eyes, concerned that Itachi had suddenly stopped speaking.

Itachi took a deep breath. "But...it's just the two of us. I'll always be there, like a wall you need to climb over."

Tell him what you've decided about him...

"Even if it means being hated, that's what big brothers are for." He looked at Sasuke with feeling in his eyes.

His little brother opened his mouth, but his words were wiped out by the sound of the door being flung open.

"Itachi, you there?! Come out! We need to talk to you!!" Yashiro's voice thundered from the entryway.

"It's all right," was all he said as he left his brother on the veranda, and turned his feet toward the front door.

On the right, Inabi; on the left, Yashiro. Behind them, Tekka stood at the ready. His father's trusted retainers.

"What is it? What brings you all here?" Itachi asked coolly, faced with the dreadful light in their eyes.

"Only two people didn't show up to yesterday's meeting." It was the long-haired Inabi who spoke first. His gaze was nothing other than hostile. "Where were you?!"

The roundabout way of speaking got Itachi's hackles up.

Only two people didn't show up to yesterday's meeting...

Itachi and Shisui.

These three already knew about Shisui's death. And on top of that, they first had to ask Itachi why he himself had been absent. Such a circuitous, pompous route to what they really wanted.

"Since joining the Anbu," Inabi continued, glaring at the still-silent Itachi, "you've pulled us through many situations. We understand that. Your father said so, too, and he's trying to defend you, but..."

Yashiro picked up where Inabi left off. "But we can't make exceptions." With these arrogant words, he placed himself above Itachi. His words existed in this series of events solely for that purpose.

Imbecile...

Itachi held back a sigh. And then he managed to spit out words, carrying the weight of his heavy heart. "I understand. I'll be careful from now on. Now, are we done here?"

If he said anything more, his rage would boil over. And if that happened, Itachi wasn't sure that he would be able to stop himself.

"Almost," Yashiro said, lowering his voice slightly. "We do have a few more questions." He was finally getting to the real point of this visit. "It's about Uchiha Shisui. He threw himself into the Nakano River last night, and killed himself."

Here we go...

"Shisui was the other person who didn't show up at the meeting," Inabi added. "And we know you adored him, like he was your own brother."

And yet, knowing that, who exactly was it who ordered Shisui to watch me? Itachi pushed back the violent feelings that threatened to turn the voice of his heart into words; it was like swallowing a steel ball. And then he selected inoffensive words, packaged in the proper appearances.

"Is that so? I haven't seen him at all lately...but what a terrible tragedy."

Their meeting alone on that cliff was a secret that no one could ever know. He had no intention of telling men as shallow as these.

At this response from Itachi, the three policemen fell silent, still glaring at him as though he were the enemy.

"Well, the Military Police Force has decided to begin a full investigation." Inabi's extremely official-sounding words broke the silence.

"...Investigation?!"

"This is Shisui's final note." Yashiro pulled out a piece of paper folded in two, and handed it to Itachi. "A handwriting analysis was conducted. There's no doubt Shisui himself wrote it."

"If there's no indication of murder, then what's the investigation for?" Itachi asked.

"For a sharingan user, copying handwriting is easy," Inabi replied.

Itachi took the note, and opened it.

"The content of his suicide note is all here on this tiny piece of paper," Yashiro remarked.

Shisui's suicide note…

The note that Itachi had written and secretly left in Shisui's room that night, ordered to do so by the dying Shisui himself. He had only been apart from it for a dozen or so hours. Even now, he had the text of it memorized. He didn't even need to look at it.

> *I'm tired of these missions.*
> *At this rate, there's no future*
> *for Uchiha.*
> *Or for me.*
> *I can't run counter to*
> *the Path any longer.*

What was the "Path" Shisui mentioned?

It was the path that each member of the clan who saw this text had in mind. He was tired of missions. The Uchihas had no future. He couldn't run counter to the Path. These sorrowful words spelled out Uchiha Shisui's pained cry, his hope to ease his clan's rage by even the smallest amount.

But it appeared his message did not reach the brethren.

"He was one of the most talented of the clan," Yashiro said. "And the best ever at teleportation. He was always the first to take on any mission for the sake of the clan."

Any mission… Did he mean monitoring Itachi?

These were the men who had handed down the cowardly order to watch one of their own, and yet they forgot their own guilt. They applauded Shisui as a capable man, but Itachi

could see, behind these fine words, that they thought of him as nothing other than a useful pawn. The flames of rage burned even more fiercely within him; their behavior was the ultimate in cowardice.

Unable to even sense this turmoil in Itachi, Inabi picked up where Yashiro left off. "It's hard to believe a man like that would leave a note like this, and kill himself."

Always thinking of yourselves...

"You shouldn't judge people by appearances or preconceptions." This was sarcasm, and also referred to himself. But there was no way these three would understand that.

"We'll leave the note with you, for the time being," Inabi continued, as though Itachi hadn't spoken. "Take it back to the Anbu, and request their cooperation in the investigation."

"Understood."

The three men turned their backs, and Itachi was relieved. If the conversation had continued even a moment longer, he probably wouldn't have been able to control his rage.

"Hopefully, we'll get some sort of lead," Yashiro spat when he crossed the threshold.

Without looking back, the silent-so-far Tekka told Itachi, "We have alternate information channels into the Anbu. If you destroy the note, we'll know."

*That's it...*Itachi clenched the hand clutching Shisui's note. "Why don't you just say it?"

About to pass through the gates, all three men stopped. When they turned around, their eyes were shining crimson. A desire for murder filled the air between the four ninjas.

He wanted nothing more.

"You think I did this?" Itachi's field of view was dyed red.

"In fact, we do, you child." Inabi said through clenched teeth.

Yashiro faced Itachi again. "Listen, Itachi," he said, murderously. "If you did indeed betray the clan, you *will* pay."

Itachi's body was faster than his voice, faster than his thoughts. He launched a kick at Yashiro's throat, caught Inabi in the face with his arm as he whirled around, and plunged his knee into the pit of Tekka's stomach. As he whirled around to face forward again, the three tumbled clumsily to the ground, and Itachi stood tall in the middle.

"Like I said, don't judge people by appearances or preconceptions."

Hit hard in vital points, the three men remained doubled over, unable to move.

"You misjudge me completely if you think I have patience for you."

Trembling, Inabi finally just barely managed to lift his head, and glare at Itachi.

"The clan...The clan...," Itachi continued. "You babble on, but you overestimate your abilities. And you have no idea of the depth of mine, which is why you're crawling right now."

On all fours, trying desperately to stand up, Yashiro looked over his shoulder at Itachi, and spat, "Shisui...had been watching you recently...It's been six months since you entered the Anbu...What you've said and done since then is too strange to overlook. What on earth are you thinking?"

"You cling to your organization, to your clan, and to your name...You limit yourself, you arbitrarily decide on your

capacity. Disgusting...and then, you fear and despise what you can't yet see...still don't know...Sheer idiocy!!" Itachi replied.

Making his father bear the brunt of it, ordering Shisui to do dirty work, hiding themselves in the shadows, squirming around in secret. Men like these did not deserve to live. And if this vanguard of the radical faction were to die, that foolish plan might also lose some of its power.

Die...

"Itachi, stop it!!"

He was about to fly at them once more, when a fierce voice from behind stopped him. He looked back to find his father standing stock still, a stunned look on his face.

"That's enough. What's wrong with you?" Without looking at the three men on the ground, his father walked straight toward him. "Itachi, I'm worried about your behavior of late."

Itachi dropped his head to avoid the visual axis of his father's sharingan. "There's nothing to worry about." *It's your behavior that's worrying...*He crushed the words in his heart with different ones. "I'm busy with work...That's all."

"Then why didn't you show up last night?" His father waited silently for Itachi's answer.

"...I needed to achieve the next state," Itachi murmured.

"What are you talking about?"

He couldn't exactly say, *I killed Shisui and got the Mangekyo sharingan.* He was angry with himself for choosing his words even in a situation like this, and that anger made his hand take up a kunai. Without even looking in that direction, he tossed the blade off toward the wall to the right. The cold tip plunged into the center of the Uchiha clan crest drawn crisply there.

Sweat sprang up on his father's brow. He turned his eyes on his son, a restless energy radiating from his body.

Itachi lowered his face. "My ability's been repressed by this pathetic clan."

Had Shisui worked so desperately, and died, to save people like this? Was this clan really worth saving? Itachi didn't know.

"Obsessing over worthless things like the clan, you lose sight of what's really important." Peace in the village. Wasn't that more important than the clan's resentment? "Premonition and imagination...You can't achieve real change as long as you're bound by regulations and restrictions."

If the clan only broke free from the fetters that bound them, they could live in harmony with the people of the village. It was pride that drove the clan, the desire to protect their small world. His father and the others couldn't see that.

"What insolence!!"

His father could only hear insolence in the cries of Itachi's heart. Once more, he was stunned by how far apart they were. So then, they would never understand each other. In which case...

In the back of his mind, a hazy image of an ominous future rose up.

"Enough!" His father glared at him, as he held the crouching Yashiro by the shoulders. "If you continue to speak this non-sense, you're going to prison!"

Nonsense...

The memory of a distant day popped into his head. The first day of class at the academy. The teacher had asked about their dreams, and Itachi had announced his to the class: *"I want to be*

the greatest ninja ever, great enough that I can erase all fighting from this world."

Everyone had thought it was nonsense. But he was still earnestly pursuing that dream, even now. *Erase all fighting from this world*... People could laugh, they could think it nonsense, but that was all Itachi truly wanted.

But his father could not see the way he suffered for this dream. Fugaku pulled his men to their feet, almost embracing them, and then they stood in front of Itachi.

"Well, what're you going to do?!" Inabi spat fiercely. "This will not be tolerated. Captain, give the arrest order!!"

Itachi could not be captured there. The four ringleaders of the coup d'état were assembled before him. Now that he had arrived here at the end of the line, all he could do was stand firm.

Shattering his resolve was his brother shouting, almost shrieking. "Itachi! Stop it!"

My brother's watching...

Sasuke had heard all of this.

Like a marionette with its strings cut, Itachi's knees folded, and he crumpled onto the stone paving of the path. He quietly put both hands on the ground, and bowed his head deeply.

I can't kill someone in front of my brother...It was his pride as the older brother. And the single-minded desire not to hurt his brother.

"I did not kill Shisui...But I apologize for my inappropriate remarks...I'm very sorry."

It was not an apology from the heart. His father likely knew that. But, as if carefully considering his son's pain, Fugaku replied, calmly, "Lately, the heavy mission load for the Anbu seems to have tired him out."

"Captain!!" Inabi cried, as if reproaching Fugaku for his weakness.

"The Anbu is under the Hokage's direct control," his father continued. "Even we can't arrest him without a warrant. As for my son...I'll take responsibility for him. Please..." His father's voice was hoarse, as he bowed his head to his subordinates.

"...Understood," Inabi said, sounding displeased.

"Itachi, inside." His father turned, and slipped through the gate.

Still on his knees, head bowed to the ground, Itachi stared after him. *What do you know?*

The flames smoldering in his heart had not been quenched. His feelings became a torrent of chakra pouring into his eyes. Itachi felt his sharingan transform.

Mangekyo...

For an instant, he met his little brother's eyes.

∞

Alone, Fugaku considered the incident of the previous day. Listening to the raindrops beating down on the roof, he sat with eyes closed and arms crossed.

He was off duty. Itachi had left on a mission, and Sasuke was at the academy. His wife had also gone out, to do the shopping. The only person in the house was Fugaku.

When they passed each other in the hallway that morning, Itachi had not greeted him. His son hadn't so much as glanced at him as he passed by, and Fugaku regretted that he hadn't been

able to reach out to Itachi then.

His dealings with Yashiro and the others, together with the kunai that had scarred the clan crest, made Itachi's position clear.

My son is with the village…

Fugaku was planning a coup d'état; this was a complication that had to be prevented at any cost. A ninja of Itachi's caliber going over to the enemy was enormous. The success or failure of the coup rested on which side could claim Itachi as its own. But Fugaku couldn't decide if it was right to force his son to bow to him.

What must Yashiro and the others have thought of a boss like him? No one would accept a captain who couldn't even make his own son fall into line. And there was still the lingering doubt about Shisui's death, further deepening Itachi's isolation within the clan.

"Excuse me?" A girl's voice interrupted Fugaku's thoughts.

*A visitor…*Standing up slowly, Fugaku stepped out of his room, and headed toward the front door.

"You…" He tried desperately to remember the name of the girl folding a wet umbrella, and looking up at him with eyes on the verge of tears. He was certain she had been in the same class as Itachi at the academy. He'd also seen her several times at the meetings.

"My name's Izumi. Uchiha Izumi," the girl said, in a forlorn voice.

He remembered now. She was the daughter of Uchiha Hazuki, who had returned to the clan after losing her husband in the Nine Tails incident. He was fairly certain that Hazuki was two years younger than he was.

"Itachi's out on a mission. I don't know when he'll be back." His words were too curt; even he thought he sounded surly.

His girlfriend?

It was hard to believe his son would have a girlfriend, given that he thought about nothing but missions. But the girl standing before his eyes was hanging her head with a pained look on her face, as though she had heard about the incident the day before. She looked as though she were devoted to his son.

"Oh, he's out? All right, I'll come another time." The girl Izumi turned around and took a step toward the door.

"Er." It was a pathetic call to stop her. Almost like he was a teenager again.

Confused, Izumi turned around.

It was all fine and good to stop her, but he didn't know what he should say. The only reason he spoke at all was simply because he felt he couldn't let her go home like that. As if to hide his discomfort, Fugaku scratched his cheek with a fingertip and told her honestly, "He's gruff, but he is kind."

"I know," Izumi replied, in an unexpectedly strong voice.

Awed by her eyes gazing directly at him, he continued. "He has few allies. I'd ask you don't abandon him."

Izumi's eyes widened.

She's a beautiful girl, he thought.

"Please."

"Don't worry," Izumi said clearly, and bowed deeply before turning her back to him, and crossing the threshold. "Sorry to have bothered you." She closed the door, and disappeared into the rainy village.

Left alone once more, Fugaku was touched by this girl's

strong heart and her feelings for his son, and he couldn't stop something warm from dampening his cheeks.

2

"Itachi's twelve now. It's about time you did it." Danzo looked down on Hiruzen, sitting at the Hokage's desk. "With Shisui's death, the only pawn we have against the Uchiha is Itachi. We can't have him spending his days burdened with all these random missions as a member of the Anbu under your control."

"Promote him to team leader, hm?"

"It's just as I said before. Raise his official age by a year, and the issue of the rules resolves itself."

Sighing, Hiruzen stretched his hands out on his desk, picking up his pipe and bringing a flame to the bowl. Purple smoke drifted up into the air. The creases around his eyes deepening, Hiruzen looked at Danzo, and said, "I can't stop feeling sorry about Shisui's death. That a ninja of his abilities would commit suicide..."

Danzo snickered in his heart. The poison Sugaru had used disappeared in the blood, so that there was no trace of it when the murder was later investigated. It was a technique befitting a member of the Foundation, where the bulk of their work was assassination. A group as dim-witted as the Military Police Force would never notice Danzo pulling strings behind the scenes.

If he had one worry, it would be Itachi. There was a possibility that he knew. The note Shisui left before he died bothered

Danzo. It was hard to believe Shisui had had so much time that he had been able to leave a note in his room before throwing himself into the river. The most likely scenario was that Itachi had copied Shisui's handwriting, and written the note. Still, Danzo could use Itachi's desire for peace to handle even this situation.

He turned to the man who was meant to be his old friend. "The Uchiha were quiet for a time because of Shisui's death, but recently, they've started to move again. We won't be able to avoid an explosion."

"I know that."

"So, then?"

"I'll approve Itachi's promotion."

The corners of Danzo's mouth naturally curled up. "Then I'll go ahead with the paperwork."

"But this is at most a special case."

Danzo responded with a nod. "When the dissatisfaction of the Uchiha clan is eliminated, I'll release Itachi."

"Once they settle down, there's no need of Itachi. After that, you do what you want."

Would that day actually ever come? In his heart, Danzo sneered at Hiruzen's softness.

∞

"In name, it's the establishment of a new team due to the increase in the number of Anbu missions. And with a new team comes a new team leader. A position you were selected for," Danzo recounted dispassionately, sitting tall before Itachi in the office of the Foundation mansion. Sugaru was standing behind

Danzo, in his usual white tiger mask. "I've asked that the members of this new team come from the Foundation, and I've obtained Hiruzen's approval."

"So then, will I belong to the Foundation?" Itachi asked.

"You won't be under the Hokage's direct command, nor will you belong to the Foundation. Let's just say this will be a special team, independent within the Anbu."

"I don't really understand what that means," Itachi said firmly.

A smile crept onto Danzo's face. "I'll spell it out." He stopped there, and stroked the area around his right eye, covered with a bandage. "The formation of a new team is just the official line. There are no new personnel. It's simply something we came up with, to allow you to move freely. Even so, I think we'll give you a couple of men."

"For the sake of the Uchiha?"

"Precisely." Danzo stood up, and walked around his desk. He came over to Itachi, and looked down on him with a lightless eye. "Saying the new members would be from the Foundation is also a means to keep the Anbu from becoming suspicious. Just like Uchiha Shisui worked for Hiruzen, you will work for me from now on."

Danzo uttered the name of Itachi's good friend, and in his smooth attitude, Itachi could see the depth of the darkness in the man standing before him. These two men had killed Shisui. Itachi had heard this directly from the dead man himself, so there was no mistake.

"Why did you kill Shisui?" Itachi asked, the pattern of the magatama popping up in his eyes.

Danzo took the sharingan in calmly and did not move, smile still on his face. "So, you did know?"

"Shisui was trying to stop the clan's coup d'état for the sake of the village. Just as he was about to do that, you interfered, and he died."

"Do you really think Shisui's actions could have stopped the coup?"

Itachi, at a loss for a reply, was ashamed of himself for faltering.

"His actions would have gotten in the way of my own plan to prevent the coup. But Shisui of the Body Flicker...even if I had ordered him not to go forward, I doubt he would have been willing to listen, given that I'm not his superior."

"And that's why you killed him?"

"It is."

Bloodlust glittered in Itachi's eyes. In an instant, his right hand was clutching a kunai, and he was thrusting it at Danzo's throat.

The man in the tiger mask blocked his way; Itachi's kunai pierced Sugaru's palm.

Over the shoulder of his loyal subordinate, Danzo started speaking. "You must have already realized it?"

"Shut up."

"How can we protect the peace of the village? And who will do what needs to be done?"

"Did you not hear me tell you to shut up?"

"If you want to kill me, then go ahead and kill me. But killing me won't stop the clan from exploding. In fact, once I'm gone, and no longer in their way, the clan will likely get more

and more carried away. And the moment you kill me, a village official, you become a criminal. Even if you were to make it out of this house, you would be pursued until you were dead. You will not be able to help your clan like that. You'll only be able to watch over the terrible spectacle from outside the village. If you wish to choose that foolish path, then go ahead and kill me."

It was a clear provocation. Danzo didn't have the slightest intention of dying. The only other person in this room was Sugaru, but scores of Danzo's people were in hiding all around them. Even if Itachi did manage to kill Danzo, it would be very nearly impossible to take all of them on, and escape from the mansion.

"Every second we stand here like this, the window of opportunity to kill me shrinks. You don't have time for questions and answers. Once decided, a ninja shifts to immediate action."

Sugaru slowly pulled out the kunai and rotated his body. He positioned himself with one leg in front, and Danzo stood tall behind him.

"May I take your silence as your answer?"

I know...

Killing Danzo would solve nothing. Quite the opposite; the situation would most certainly deteriorate. Itachi had a bigger ambition that he had to put ahead of his personal grudge, and his desire to get vengeance for his friend. He tucked his kunai away in his vest.

"Now then, Uchiha Itachi." Danzo nodded, seemingly satisfied. "Shall we return to the issue at hand?"

"I'm leaving," Itachi said, and turned his back to Danzo.

"You can't bear to listen to any more? So it appears you *do* see it, then."

Itachi started walking toward the door.

"If someone from outside the clan did *that*, there would certainly be lingering ill will toward the village. Other clans would fear the Uchiha end, and one would inevitably become the next Uchiha. Which is exactly why..."

Ignoring the man, Itachi reached for the door.

"Someone from the clan must do it," Danzo continued. "A mentally deranged young person of the clan. If this is what everyone believes, then peace can come to the village."

Itachi opened the door with a trembling hand, and glared at Danzo over his shoulder.

"You are the only one who can fulfill this role," Danzo asserted.

As if to reject Danzo's declaration, Itachi left the room.

∞

He walked out of the Foundation mansion, and walked along the village road at the foot of the Hokage Monument.

The sound of wings. Insects.

"Don't play this stupid game. How about you just show yourself already?" Itachi announced to the sky, sunlight spilling through the trees. The branches above his head shook, and a human form dropped down before his eyes.

"Hello," Sugaru said lightly.

"What do you want?"

"I wanted to talk to you for a minute."

"On Danzo's orders?"

"It is on my own discretion." Sugaru put a hand on his white

tiger mask. As Itachi watched silently, he quietly pulled it off.

"So it is you, then."

"Yes, it is me."

He had seen this face before, with that smile creeping across it. When Tenma died and Shinko quit being a ninja after the mission to guard the daimyo of the Land of Fire, they had been replaced. One of those replacements was a girl who talked a lot. And the other was a boy who never spoke at all.

"I forget your name from that time."

"Yoji."

"That's right." The man before his eyes was the genin, Yoji.

"Just ten from the Foundation cover the entire population of Konohagakure. And another two for the Uchiha clan," the unmasked Sugaru noted.

"What are you talking about?"

"Monitoring. Separate from the Hokage's Anbu, there is a monitoring division through the Foundation solely for the Foundation."

It was only natural that Danzo's organization would have such a division in place.

"A total of twelve people are required to monitor the people of the village. With just that number of personnel, we can know the movements of the village."

Itachi couldn't believe Sugaru had stopped him to boast about the excellence of his own organization. He was not done speaking. Itachi stayed silent, and waited for Sugaru to continue.

"There is one more person who has been ordered to monitor." Sugaru's index finger thrust up into the air, rotated slowly in space, and pointed to his own chin. "Me."

"And what exactly are you monitoring?"

CHAPTER 6

"You. Ever since you started at the academy, I have been watching the person known as Uchiha Itachi."

Itachi wasn't surprised. He'd had a strange feeling since the day of his graduation ceremony, when Danzo spoke to him. Something like déjà-vu, the feeling that he'd known the man for a long time. If Danzo had started watching him when he entered the academy, then this feeling made sense.

"Lord Danzo has used twelve people to monitor the village. The fact that I was devoted to you alone is proof of just how much he has favored you."

"I'm not exactly pleased to have that man favor me."

"It seems I misspoke. You are already in the palm of Lord Danzo's hand. You won't be able to escape from his darkness."

"Did you come all this way just to tell me this nonsense?"

"My father was an extremely terrible man, you see?"

The conversation had suddenly flown off in another direction, but Itachi simply waited for Sugaru to continue.

"He was jealous of the fact that his son excelled. He was a man who could only show off his own power by hating, and causing pain. He would assault me for any reason, or no reason, so I knew how to forget pain from before I can remember."

The hard quality of Sugaru's voice as he indifferently told this tale was excessively disturbing.

"It was my fifth birthday. I accidentally fell off my chair, and spilled juice on the clothing of my father, sitting in front of me. That day, my father was likely in a terribly bad mood. 'Your apology sounded cheeky,' he said, and slit my throat." His voice gradually grew heavier and darker. "It was then that I killed someone for the first time."

ITACHI'S STORY
[MIDNIGHT]

"Is your voice an after-effect of that?"

"No," Sugaru said, waving his right hand. "Because of my father, I completely lost my voice. It was only after Lord Danzo took me in that I learned how to speak by making the insects I keep on my body make a small noise in resonance."

The rustling voice was the product of combining the quiet noises of insects.

"People have darkness within them. I learned that when I was five years old. However, the darkness I carry is still slight, compared with that of Lord Danzo. My darkness is a personal darkness. But his darkness is the darkness of this village. If you kill him now, the darkness that fills that body will spill out all at once, into the village. And if that happens, this village will not be able to remain sane."

"So, you're telling me not to kill him, or something?"

"Right now, you could not kill him."

"I won't know unless I try—"

"I know." Sugaru cut him off, as if to beat him to the punch. "You are not sufficiently ready."

Itachi said nothing.

"You are prepared to shoulder the darkness of your clan."

They glared at each other, neither moving an inch. Only the dry conversation went back and forth in the space between them.

"Do you know a child called Naruto?"

"The jinchuriki for Nine Tails."

"Though imperfect, he is the son of the fourth Hokage. Don't you think it strange that because Nine Tails is housed in that body, everyone in the village treats him so cruelly?"

"Danzo?"

"Yes." The narrow eyes on Sugaru's pale face bent into bow-like arcs as he smiled. "Human beings are cowardly creatures who obtain their own emotional stability as they sympathize with or slander people lower than themselves, foolish people."

"Are all human beings—"

"I know," Sugaru said simply, cutting Itachi off. And then, he continued matter-of-factly, faint smile still on his face. "Someone like you, born under a warrior star, is different. You'd best not think that everyone is as strong as you are."

Itachi wanted to be strong, he wanted to be a warrior, but he had never once thought that he was.

"Lord Danzo did one thing. He simply made it known that the Nine Tails that plunged the village into terror was housed in the body of that child. The people of the village then made their own judgments, and decided on their own to discriminate against Naruto. With this terrifying child as their just cause, they shifted responsibility to someone else, and now the people turn a cold shoulder to Naruto. And by looking down on the poor child, they maintain their emotional equilibrium. Your clan fulfills a similar role to Naruto. Isn't that so?"

"Are you saying that Danzo's pulling the strings behind the discrimination against the clan, too?"

"That is an enmity from before Lord Danzo was born. It's not good to make everything his fault."

Itachi was forced to move with the slippery Sugaru. He might try to change the flow of the conversation, but he couldn't catch hold of an opening.

"Sacrifice Naruto's life, and reduce dissatisfaction in the vil-

LAGE. SACRIFICE THE UCHIHA CLAN, AND MAINTAIN PUBLIC ORDER. THE DIS-SATISFACTION OF THE VARIOUS PEOPLE THAT ARISES IN THE VILLAGE ACCUMU-LATES IN LORD DANZO HIMSELF. ALL RESPONSIBILITY LIES WITH HIM. THAT MAN IS PREPARED TO SHOULDER THE DARKNESS OF THE VILLAGE. ARE YOU PREPARED TO DO THAT MUCH, AT LEAST, UCHIHA ITACHI?"

Prepared to shoulder the darkness produced through sacrifice... For Itachi at that moment, those words were heavier than anything else. Had he actually taken on the darkness produced by the sacrifice of his friend's death?

"ALL THE SAME, YOU CANNOT KILL LORD DANZO. AND YOU MOST CER-TAINLY CANNOT ESCAPE HIM." Sugaru's words dragged Itachi into the darkness. "REMEMBER THIS—AT ANY MOMENT, I AM WATCHING YOU."

Sugaru's body transformed into countless insects, and flew upward. An infinity of black dots bled into the light filtering through the trees, which had started to take on a crimson hue.

Once the insects had disappeared, Itachi turned his head to the sky. "Shisui. What should I do?" He had never prayed for the existence of God like he did at that moment.

"Answer me, Shisui."

His friend's spirit did not begin speaking to him, nor did the hand of God reach down to save him.

3

In the small, dark room, a man in a monkey mask was sit-ting in front of Itachi. He carried out his duties matter-of-factly, processing the mountain of documents piled on the desk. Papers covered in dense text, papers that looked like blueprints. There were also some pages with photos of faces attached to them. All were documents related to the Uchiha clan.

Itachi was in the room given to him in the Foundation mansion.

"It's been a year since then. Time flies, hm?" the man in the monkey mask said. His voice sounded like he was still just barely twenty.

Itachi had known the face under the mask since he was little. He had seen it any number of times since the Uchiha clan was forcibly moved to the compound on the edge of the village.

Uchiha Kagen. Itachi had only learned his name once they started working together. Kagen was an unremarkable man, in a logistical operations division in the Military Police Force. His rank was genin, and he didn't have any particularly spectacular techniques. At the meetings, he never voiced his own thoughts, but rather, always followed the opinions of other people.

Or that's what I thought, anyway...

The man before his eyes was a member of the Foundation. The real Kagen was dead. The man before him had a twin, a little brother with the same physique and chakra. The two had both been given Kagen's face. These twins were the Foundation members Sugaru had said were investigating the movements of the clan.

The fact that Kagen worked in a logistics division meant that he hadn't had any opportunities to activate the sharingan. Thus, due to the fact that during his lifetime, he had been thoroughly unremarkable, and the fact that he had no close relatives, no one suspected anything when he was secretly replaced. The roots of

the village reached that deeply into the Uchiha clan.

The real name of the man in the monkey mask was Gozu. His younger brother was Mezu.

The "since then" Gozu was talking about was the death of Shisui.

"Because Shisui died, the radical faction was forced to revise their plan, and postpone the day of action. So his death delayed the coup d'état, which is a bit of irony, hm?" The older Gozu was using a more polite form of speech because Itachi was his superior.

The subordinates given to Itachi after Danzo made him an Anbu team leader were Gozu and Mezu. Isolated from the other Anbu teams, Itachi's role was to watch the Uchiha clan very closely, along with these two men.

"They were going to use Shisui's teleportation to charge the Residence and abduct the third Hokage. That was the basic idea. So, I suppose it is only natural that Shisui's death would slow their movements."

"Quit babbling, and do your job," Itachi said, running his eyes over Yashiro's revised plan for the coup d'état.

Just as Gozu had noted, one of the key elements of the plan put together by his father and the others was the abduction of the third Hokage. The Military Police Force would strike a blow against the village ninjas by kidnapping their leader. Those ninjas would attack them, and they would fight back, buying time and forcing the village to accept the demands of the clan. That was the overall concept of the coup.

Their demands were four: Uchiha participation in the center of the village, dismantling of the compound, the freedom to choose where they lived, and Uchiha Fugaku named as the fifth Hokage.

Itachi couldn't believe the village would accept such impossible demands, but the members of the radical faction seriously intended to push them.

"As noted in the revised draft you are reading, Team Leader, it seems that they have come up with an idea for abducting the Hokage that doesn't require Shisui. They should start to move again soon, yes?" Gozu said calmly, not bothered in the slightest by Itachi's rebuke.

Itachi lifted his eyes from the document in his hand, and glared at his subordinate. "Such impertinence."

Silly monkey mask in place, Gozu shrugged his shoulders exaggeratedly, like a clown.

"Team Leader!" A shrill cry came from the door.

"Hey, Mezu! How was your watch?" Gozu asked the man in the doorway.

On Mezu's face was a monkey mask just like Gozu's. The only difference was the color of the markings. Gozu's were red, while Mezu's were blue. In the compound, one of them would pretend to be Kagen, and watch over the clan. Gozu being here meant that Mezu had to be in the compound.

"No time for that. They're moving, Team Leader." Mezu's tone was somewhat rougher than Gozu's, as he turned his monkey mask to Itachi and began to speak. "There's a clan meeting today, and apparently, Fugaku's going to tell everyone the date of the action and their assignments."

"Did you know that, Team Leader?" Gozu's asked, and Itachi shook his head from side to side.

The time to come has finally come...

This was the thought that replayed in Itachi's mind. Shisui's death had only put off the coup. At some point, the clan would begin to move again. He wasn't alone in thinking this; Gozu and Mezu were with him there; Danzo and the other village officials also shared his view.

As Itachi kept his two subordinates in check with his eyes, his lips trembled faintly. "I knew that there was a meeting today, but I didn't know what it was about."

He had barely spoken with his father since the incident with Yashiro and the others, and he had stopped showing up at the meetings. Itachi honestly knew nothing, other than what he discovered here with his team.

"You're the one going to the meeting, right?" Mezu said, looking at Gozu.

The monkey mask with the red coloring nodded.

"I see." The words abruptly slipped out of Itachi's mouth. "Time to move, then." Up to that point, he had deliberately run from it. From facing the clan head on.

This was his last opportunity.

∞

Itachi steeled himself, and opened the door. All eyes turned to him at once.

"Why are you here?" a man sitting deep inside the room asked, in a voice filled with malice. Yashiro.

"I came to talk."

"What do you have to say at this late date?" Beside Yashiro,

Inabi stood up and faced Itachi. "Hm, Itachi?"

The room fell silent. Looking out into that quiet, he found Izumi. She was staring at him with a look on her face like she was about to start crying.

"Stop this foolishness," he said, honestly.

As Inabi glared at him, Inabi's right eyebrow shot upward and twitched. "And what foolishness is that?"

"The coup d'état."

Everyone started talking at once. The only person in the room looking at him with cool eyes was Gozu, now Kagen.

Following Inabi, Yashiro also stood up. "You don't even come to the meetings. Nothing you can say will change anything now."

"The village is not as soft as you think it is."

"We're not kids like you." A blue vein popped up on Yashiro's forehead. "We're more than well aware of the fact that the village is not soft. That's why we've endured this situation for as long as we have."

"If you fight them, you'll lose."

"Quiet!" his father roared, still seated at the front of the room. The room froze instantly at his tremendous rage. "Anyone who says they will lose without even trying is not qualified to be a ninja. Leave this place."

As if rejecting his father's words, Itachi stayed where he was.

"Out!" The roar also did not yield.

"Do you really believe you can win, Father?" Itachi asked calmly.

After a brief silence, his father began speaking, choosing his words carefully. "You are still young. You do not know the true

face of this world. There is a reality that cannot be changed, no matter how one might struggle in the face of it. You still do not understand just how empty life is, when you must simply continue to endure something until death."

"If that reality is so empty, then change it."

"That's exactly what we're trying to do!!" Yashiro interrupted the exchange between father and son.

"By relying on a foolish plan that doesn't even examine the possibility of failure?"

"How much of a fool must you try to make of us before you're satisfied, Itachi?! You think too much of yourself. Show some respect! However talented you might be, I will not permit any further mockery!"

"Be quiet a moment, Yashiro."

"Captain!"

"I am speaking with my son." Fugaku—"Wicked Eye"— glared at Yashiro with a murderous sharingan.

His hot-blooded subordinate sat, trembling, a look of dissatisfaction on his face.

"Itachi." Taking the opportunity of Yashiro's silence, his father began to speak once again. "Winning or losing is secondary; the fact that we acted is key. When we act, the people of the village will know the discrimination we Uchihas have been subject to. Then they will fear us, and the village will change."

"You are already feared. That's why the clan was gathered together in one place, and driven to the edge of the village."

"That was the vague fear of the Nine Tails' attack; this time, it will be a fear accompanied by real pain. The nature of it is different."

"That's splitting hairs."

"Why won't you understand?" A deep crease of sorrow was carved out between his father's eyebrows. "I am acting for you, and for your children. My generation will change the way the Uchihas are currently ostracized."

You... He meant Itachi and Sasuke. And their children would be his grandchildren.

"If you're thinking about us, then why would you do something this foolish—" Itachi's voice was choked, while his ears picked up hard words muttered by the group around him.

"Traitor sure talks big."

"Get out."

"Right. Get out!"

In the blink of an eye, the angry voices joined together to form a massively powerful wave. All of it hatred, focused on Itachi. His father could no longer do anything to stop the vortex of anger that had become the consensus of the clan.

Itachi lost the will to say anything else.

It's come this far, then...

He slowly turned his back to his father. And then he walked lifelessly toward the door he himself had left open.

"Wait!" Izumi's voice came at Itachi from behind.

Although he stopped, he couldn't muster the energy to turn around.

Running over to him, Izumi came around to stand in front of him, and grabbed his shoulders. "It's all right. It'll be all right," she said desperately, her eyes shining red.

"If you don't go back, they'll think you're a traitor too, you know."

"I don't care what anyone thinks."

Izumi's voice held a sob, and he felt it only too painfully.

"Talk to them one more time. If you really talk to them, they'll understand."

"It's no good."

"But it's just, like this..."

Itachi stepped back, peeling her shaking hands off his shoulders, and started walking again without looking at her.

"They're already where they are."

"Itachi..." She didn't come after him again.

He walked home alone on a road shrouded in darkness. The compound was silent, since the majority of the clan was taking part in the meeting.

A man was leaning against the wall he could see out of the corner of his eye.

Monkey mask... Mezu's, with the blue coloring.

Itachi stopped when he was in front of Mezu, his eyes still turned toward his destination.

"End of the line... That's it, huh?"

Itachi continued to stare straight ahead, not responding.

"I wonder exactly how they're gonna pin down the third Hokage aka the Professor, huh? Heh, heh, heh..." Mezu's mean laughter drifted off into the night; then, apparently discomfited by the unresponsive Itachi, he cleared his throat, becoming serious. "Isn't it about time we have to report the results of our investigation to the senior officials?"

"I know," Itachi replied, briefly, and started walking again.

Among all the stars glittered in the heavens, only the moon was not visible.

4

"This can no longer be tolerated!" The first to open her mouth after hearing Itachi's report was Utatane Koharu.

An interrogation room in the Hokage Residence, used when the four ninjas who comprised the village executive were receiving critical reports. Four black chairs were set up at the long table, and seated in them, from right to left, were Mitokado Homura, the third Hokage, Utatane Koharu, and Danzo.

Itachi had requested an emergency meeting to report on the current clan situation, which he had been investigating together with Gozu and Mezu in the year since he had been made team leader, as well as the details of the incident at the meeting the previous day.

According to Gozu, who had remained at the meeting after Itachi left, the details of the plot had been made known.

The date for the coup d'état is ten days from now... The plan was to begin with the Hokage attack team led by Yashiro.

"If they are calling for revolution, and intending to usurp the government, then we will be forced to declare the Uchiha traitors to Konoha."

"Koharu, stop! Don't get ahead of things," Hiruzen chided the imperious older woman.

Danzo stared at him with a cool gaze. "But, Hiruzen," he said, quietly. "The Uchiha clan can no longer be stopped. In which case, in order to avoid chaos, we must strike as soon as possible...That also means the children, who know nothing of this plot."

"That is not something to be said in front of Itachi!" Hiruzen snapped, as Itachi simply watched. The fox mask on his face looked out into empty space.

On the surface, Hiruzen's words could have been taken as a kindness, but hidden in them was also proof that the Hokage was thinking the same thing as Danzo. Hiding ugly things from people's eyes like this was the true nature of this village.

"And if it comes to civil war with the Uchihas, it will be no simple matter," Hiruzen continued. "We must have some kind of plan."

Exactly how seriously has he thought about the Uchihas?

Itachi had his doubts about Hiruzen. Despite his concerns of civil war, he hadn't once come to speak directly with Fugaku and the others. And it was Hiruzen who had removed Shisui from his regular duties, and allowed him to maneuver in secret. On the surface, he spoke as if from the heart, but in making Itachi independent as a team leader, so he could continuously monitor the clan, Hiruzen was doing the same thing as Danzo.

The discussion continued.

"It is a race against time." Danzo around looked at the others. "We must strike first, before they can act. If you and I join together, along with our Anbu, for a surprise attack from behind, it will soon be over."

"The Uchiha were our comrades-in-arms...Rather than force, I'd like to try talking with them."

Why didn't you show that determination sooner? It's too late now, Itachi murmured to himself.

"I'll think of a plan," Hiruzen told Danzo, and then abruptly turned his eyes on Itachi. "Itachi. Buy us as much time as possible. Every little bit helps."

Wasn't there a man who had already given his life to buy that "as much time as possible?" The old people here had simply wasted the year Shisui traded his life to produce, instead of working out some concrete plan. The coup was in ten days. What would buying any more time for these old people accomplish?

"Understood."

"We're counting on you, Itachi."

Distress bleeding into it, the hoarse voice of Hiruzen, forced to go against his own true feelings, sounded hollow to the ears of Itachi.

∞

"Hiruzen might have said all that, but when push comes to shove, he'll protect Konoha. He's that kind of man. And when push does come to shove, he'll have to take firm measures as the Hokage," Danzo told Itachi quietly, as they stood in the courtyard of the Foundation mansion.

Danzo's soul hadn't stopped shaking since hearing Itachi's report.

The coup, in ten days. The time had come at last. He would finally be able to remove the biggest obstacle threatening the security of the village. Danzo trembled with glee at being able to personally put an end to the history of enmity that went back to the founding of Konoha.

Itachi listened silently. He was a clever boy. In the interrogation room, he had seen it in Hiruzen's attitude, so replete with self-righteousness and hypocrisy. He had already grasped

Danzo's true intentions. Or rather, the idea had sprouted in Itachi's own heart when his brethren accused him of the death of his good friend Shisui. That idea was now simply overlaid on the image Danzo had spent long years drawing.

Yes. The two of them standing in that spot at the moment were of one mind.

"Whether it turns into a war or not," Danzo began calmly, looking at the silent Itachi, "at the moment the coup occurs, the fate of the Uchihas will be annihilation."

The plan the Uchihas had put together was simply too crude. Swept away in a flood of emotion, they overestimated their own power. To him, their plan was like a sad little poem written by a sentimentalist despairing of this world, and ending his own life.

He did find it a little sad that the genius Itachi had been born into such a sorry clan. But no one could escape fate. At the moment he was born an Uchiha, Itachi's path was set.

The path of destruction...

Danzo readied himself to scatter the bait. "Including your little brother, who knows nothing of all this. But if it's before the coup, there is a way to save your brother, at least."

Itachi might have done it even without the bait. That was how strong the faith of the boy in front of him appeared. He had tried so very seriously to realize his outrageous dream of eliminating war from this world. That sentimentalism was the Uchiha clan. Given that he held this anti-war conviction so firmly, perhaps Itachi would have accepted Danzo's proposal even without the bait of his younger brother's life. But Danzo was the sort of man who took every precaution. And Itachi's brother's life, in compensation for the extermination of the Uchiha, was too good of a deal.

What on earth did Itachi think of a cowardly act like threatening his younger brother? His face was frozen, impossible to read; the boy did not so much as twitch.

This was the time to strike. If he had the leeway to inquire into Itachi's mental state, then he must strike without stopping.

"Once it actually happens, your brother will learn about everything. If he sees his clan obliterated by the ninjas of Konoha, he will come to nurture a desire for vengeance on the village." First, focus Itachi's thoughts on Sasuke. Then turn Itachi's eyes away from his brethren's obliteration, and give him a just cause, in the name of saving his little brother's life. "Once that happens, there'll be nothing left but to have your brother die."

"...Is that a threat?" Itachi was indeed not to be dealt with by ordinary means.

"No. I want you to choose." Push it. "Will you side with the Uchihas, carry out the coup, and be destroyed with your clan? Or will you side with us in Konoha, and obliterate the Uchihas before the coup, leaving only your brother alive?"

From Itachi's actions up to that point, it was unthinkable that he would side with the clan. So then, why was he in such conflict over it? Was even a man of Itachi's caliber afraid of the infamy that would come with killing his clan?

"Whatever we have to do, we must get this situation under control before things descend into chaos, for the sake of the village. This mission can only be given to a double agent for both Uchiha and Konoha. There is only you, Itachi."

Itachi himself would have known that. If someone from outside the clan were put to the task of annihilating the Uchihas,

the other clans in the village would be dissatisfied with the village officials. If people started to suspect that whole clans would be purged if they were determined to be a liability to the village, the situation would become untenable. Which was exactly why the annihilation of the Uchihas needed to be done by someone in that clan. A mentally troubled boy killing his family, and his clan...this was the way to get the situation neatly under control.

"Itachi, this is likely a painful mission for you. However, in exchange, you will be able to make sure your brother survives."

Since the Hokage Residence, Itachi had said almost nothing. Even at that moment, he was staring at Danzo in silence.

Anguish...Even as he had the thought that this was not a fitting word for this boy, Danzo felt in Itachi's silence a surge of emotion that could even have been sorrow.

"I feel the same as you about the village." Danzo took a small breath before uttering his final words. "Will you...accept this mission?"

As if no longer able to endure the feelings that threatened to crush him, Itachi closed his eyes and stuck his chin out slightly. He turned his back, and started to walk.

Danzo stared, without moving a single muscle, until the departing Itachi disappeared from sight. As if to pour his own passions into him...

∞

Itachi pressed his forehead to the place on the cliff Shisui had leapt from, and pressed his eyes tightly shut. In his field of view, now shrouded in darkness, visions popped up and disappeared.

Corpses...
Rain...
Father...
And me...

Itachi was four years old. As the enormous conflict known as the Third Shinobi World War was drawing to a close, he had faced the battlefield his father brought him to. He still remembered clearly the mountain of dead bodies, no longer identifiable as ally or enemy. None of the corpses had been seeking their own death. Faces frozen, stretched out in terror or sadness, they seemed on the verge of calling out the futility of it. The young Itachi could do nothing. He had simply stood in the middle of the countless ninjas who had met untimely deaths, and cursed his own lack of power.

Ever since that day...

His thinking had changed completely.

Fighting was foolish. War must never happen. No matter how the darkness of people tried to darken him, this thinking had turned into light to illuminate the path he was to go down. It was why Itachi had made it this far.

Even after the blow to his heart after learning of his father's plot, and the clan's desire for battle. Even when his best friend had faced his own untimely death, torn between the village and the clan. Even if he ended up bringing about the demise of the clan with his own hands...

"Hngh." A sob slipped out from between his clenched teeth. Trickling along his closed eyelids, tears spilled out, and wet the dry rock. The tears he had never shown anyone.

Itachi had lived his life with the vow in his heart to become

the best ninja in the world, and for him, the act of crying was an act of defeat. Eliminating all fighting in the world was synonymous with becoming the best ninja in the world. He had no need of weakness on the road toward his outrageous dream. His dream was too big to be realized unless he was always strong, always facing forward, always walking intently toward his goal.

And yet, his tears would not stop.

Twelve years of life in this world. Itachi had almost no memories of crying. He had been a reasonable child from the time he was very little, so he didn't cry and trouble his parents. He hadn't cried when Tenma was killed, and he had activated his sharingan.

Memories of crying...

Four years old on the battlefield, and one more. The day he had killed Shisui. That time, too, it had been in this place.

"Shisui..." Itachi wondered what on earth Shisui would have said if he had been alive there.

Obliterating the clan...

Would Shisui have forgiven him? Probably not.

Shisui would have tried to protect the clan to the end. In which case, they would have ended up enemies. Maybe it was fortunate that they parted that day as friends.

Right... Itachi had already made up his mind. He had had a feeling, somehow, that this time would come, from the moment his friend died a year earlier, and he lost hope in the clan—from the instant those evil feelings sprang up in his heart.

The insurrection of the clan, chaos in the village, and then civil war...

Other villages would invade to take advantage of the

ruined Konohagakure. Fighting begat fighting, and a new Shinobi World War would break out. At the center of this chain of hatred was the Uchiha clan.

"You should stay true to your thinking. Fight, be confused, be lost, and come through that to find your answer. And once you find it, make your decision, and do not waver from it. Find your answer, and be ready to follow through. That is determination."

His father's words came back to life in his mind. Determination. The decision he was about to make was a parting from the clan. And...

A parting from his father.

He wavered. He had been lost all this long time. He had also always stared at Shisui's back, and regretted his own foolishness. Maybe there was a better way.

But...

"This is the best move," Itachi murmured, as if to convince himself. The chill in his own words made his heart constrict painfully. A lamentation wet the darkness.

When he returned home that day, his family was already asleep.

5

The Foundation mansion, Danzo's living room.

"I'll do it."

The only one who heard Itachi's words was Danzo. He stood up from the chair behind his desk, and approached Itachi

with heavy steps.

"I felt certain you would say that," he said. The hand he put on Itachi's shoulder was ridiculously cold. "Don't worry about your brother. Even after you disappear, the village will take care of him."

Itachi was going to slaughter his clan. Even if it were a mission, it was the sort that could never be made public. To the outside world, Itachi would be a criminal who had gone mad, and murdered his entire clan. Naturally, he would not be able to stay in the village. At that point, he had no choice but to believe even the words of a man like Danzo.

"The day will be the day before the planned date of the coup. How does that sound?"

Itachi had correctly understood his intentions. The mission this time was a surprise strike. A sneak attack, to wipe out a clan that suspected nothing. The night before the coup, the members of the clan would refrain from going out, in order to build up their courage and make their preparations. It was easy to see what they would do. Additionally, their thoughts would be full of the next day's action, so it shouldn't even occur to them that they would be ambushed.

"Understood."

"I'll tell Hiruzen you're desperately trying to reconcile them with the village."

Itachi had made his decision, and he had no intention of continuing this chat with Danzo. He had some ideas about his brother, too. Everything was after this mission was over.

He would take on the crime of murdering his clan for the sake of peace in the village. He despaired at himself for not being able to come up with any other way. This whole time, he had been thinking about how he would ever be able to apologize to Shisui, after his friend had entrusted him with the future.

*A decision born of failure...*That was the truth. *Nothingness...*

No matter how he dug around in his heart, no emotions appeared. Whatever he saw, whatever he heard, his heart was dead.

"What will I do about Uchiha Kagen?" The person from the clan who Gozu and Mezu played.

"Oh." Danzo opened his mouth, looking as though he had just remembered them. "One of them will have to die. If you see Kagen, go ahead and kill him."

"Are you sure?"

"The ninjas of the Foundation do not fear even death for the sake of their missions. Gozu and Mezu would both gladly die. Do not hesitate. If anyone other than you is missing from the Uchiha clan, your actions will have been for naught. At that time, I won't be able to guarantee your brother's life," Danzo added threateningly. He apparently had serious doubts about Itachi's determination. The almost pathetic suspicions of a man who did not know the word "trust."

"Understood."

"Good."

Itachi turned his back to Danzo, and started walking. When he put his hand on the door, he heard a voice from behind.

"Best if we do not meet again before your mission is complete. This is the last time I will speak with you as a ninja of Konohagakure. You have worked hard for the village up to now. I thank you."

Ignoring Danzo's uncharacteristic words, Itachi slipped through the doorway, and closed the door behind him.

"I will be a Konohagakure ninja until I die," he murmured to himself in the hallway, gloomy even at midday.

∞

Hiding from the monitoring cameras of the Anbu, Itachi stared at the grounds of Nakano Shrine, visible below him from one of the trees in the grove. He chose one with a good shape, so as to hide himself among the dense foliage.

The coup d'état was drawing near. Three more days. There was something he absolutely had to take care of before then. Itachi had been watching over Nakano Shrine ever since he left Danzo, and he had the feeling he was about to see the fruits of that labor.

The door to the main building opened, and a man stepped out, and scanned the surrounding area. He had white hair.

"Yashiro." Itachi murmured the name of the man walking furtively toward the gates.

Without waiting for him to disappear, Itachi came to stand in front of the closed door. He easily opened the lock, and stepped inside so quickly the cameras couldn't see him.

Don't go anywhere just yet, he prayed silently to the man who was his target.

He deftly pulled up the seventh tatami mat from the far right, revealing stairs that led to the basement. The secret meeting place. He ran down, and pulled open once more the door he had closed a few days earlier, the hateful voices of his brethren raining down on him.

"Hm?"

In the very back of the meeting hall, there was a stone monument with the history of the Uchiha clan carved into it. The man he was after was standing in front of it. A man in an orange mask.

"Uchiha Itachi."

"It's been a while." It was their first meeting since the time Tenma was killed.

"Four years since then. You've grown quite a bit," the man in the mask said, spreading his arms.

"Did you instigate them?"

"That's no way to talk to someone. I simply taught them a little thing about the history of their clan."

"What are you up to, Uchiha Madara?"

"Oh, ho!" The man in the mask put his hand to his chin. "You never know when someone's going to come down here. And the compound is watched by those fellows in the village. How about we go somewhere else, and talk a little?"

"All right."

Hearing this, the man's body was sucked into the holes in his mask, and reappeared behind Itachi.

"Follow me." The man climbed the stairs up to the main shrine, and went outside. Perhaps he knew the precise locations of the clearly hidden cameras; he headed straight out of the compound as if choosing a path in their blind spots, and then easily slipped past even the eyes watching the village, to step beyond it.

Once they had gone a little ways from Konohagakure, the road that led to Sunagakure came into view. There was a small

shrine in one corner, and a vast forest spread out as if to guard it. Once he had cloaked himself in these woods, the man stopped running.

The moon hanging above the grove of cedar trees was slightly distorted, on the verge of being a perfect circle.

"How do you know who I am?" the man in the mask asked, putting his hands on his hips. Behind those words was the acknowledgement that he was indeed Madara.

"You...You made it past the Konoha guard, and were looking at the secret stone of Nakano Shrine. Only the Uchiha know its location."

He had first noticed the man's existence when he was on duty monitoring the clan for the Anbu. Since then, Itachi had seen that shimmering in space within the compound any number of times. It was of the exact same nature as what he saw when Tenma died. Which is how he knew that the man before him was interfering.

"I looked into you... I took the opportunity to investigate what kind of person you were, how you thought."

As a result of which, Itachi had learned that the man before his eyes was Uchiha Madara. Seventy years ago, Madara had supposedly died after a fierce battle with the first Hokage, Senju Hashirama, but no one had actually confirmed that death. With the attack on the daimyo of the Land of Fire four years earlier, and his sniffing around the clan compound, Itachi had sensed Madara had an attachment to the village that was related to the Uchihas. And then, that evening, he had learned that Yashiro was meeting with him, and Itachi's suspicion turned into certainty.

"Well then, this will go quickly," the man in the mask started. "So, you know I am a member of the Uchiha clan, and I harbor hatred for both Konoha and Uchiha."

Uchiha Madara had resolved to fight back against the Senju clan when they tried to discriminate against the Uchihas. However, the people of the clan had ostracized Madara, who sought battle, and betrayed him, although he had been their leader. Struck by despair, Madara had fought Hashiramu alone, and then allegedly died. He would no doubt have had held an extraordinary grudge against both Konoha and Uchiha. If he had indeed been pushing Yashiro and the radical faction toward a coup d'état, it would have been to get revenge on Konoha.

However, Itachi could not allow him to take this revenge on Konohagakure.

"I have conditions." He cut through Madara's arrogant attitude. "I help you get revenge on the Uchiha clan. And in exchange, you don't lay a hand on the village. Or Uchiha Sasuke, too." He would force the point of the spear turned toward the village back toward the clan.

Madara laughed slightly, unable to hide his surprise at Itachi's forcefulness. "And what if I were to refuse?" he asked, his masked head cocked to one side.

His face devoid of all expression, Itachi offered the answer he had prepared. "If you refuse this request, then you and I are enemies."

"Could you kill me?"

"It's not a matter of whether or not I could. I *will* kill you." He had already taken a step down a road that would not allow him to turn back. He did not hesitate.

Silence enveloped them. There was no bloodlust in either of their auras. They were exchanging dangerous words, but they both acknowledged each other as opponents.

"You seem to have the wrong idea. That brat is not a friend, or anything of the like," Madara said, raising his palms to the heavens. "That brat" was Yashiro. "I tossed several stones. It just happens that one of them landed in a very good place. It wouldn't be a bad thing to change my mind now. Actually..." The small openings of darkness in the mask caught hold of Itachi, and did not let go. "Choosing you seems more interesting than those small fry in the village."

Small fry... Itachi agreed in his heart that perhaps they were small fry; in the next instant, Sasuke's face popped into his mind, and he felt a sharp pain in his heart.

"I like this tale you tell. I'll come along for the ride."

Itachi shifted his eyes as if to ignore the hand that was extended.

6

Itachi carefully took his shoes off in the entryway. His mission that day would seriously change his life. He wouldn't be taking his shoes off here anymore. The peaceful times would also end that day.

That's fine... He was prepared to bear the weight of the crime.

"Itachi." Sasuke stopped Itachi as he was about to step up into the house with an almost innocent cry, as if to keep him here in this house, in this clan.

Itachi decided to stay just a little longer in this peaceful place. Once he took that step forward, he would never be able to come back here. He moved his feet back into the entryway, and turned toward his brother.

"Help me with my shuriken today, please..."

A request he would never be able to grant again. If he was honest with himself, all he wanted to do was help Sasuke forever and ever. He had prayed for the day when his little brother would become a full-fledged ninja, and they would go on missions together. That, too, was a wish that could no longer be granted.

Struggling for a reply, he managed to give voice to a polite lie. "I'm busy... Why don't you ask Father?"

"But you're better at shuriken. Even I can tell that." His brother pouted, arms crossed behind his back, head hanging slightly.

Now that Itachi thought about it, he had used being busy as a pretext to distance himself from his brother. He wished he had spent more time with him, but what was done was done.

"Why do you always treat me like I'm such a pest?"

No... That's what he wanted to say. But that was a word he definitely could not give voice to, because soon, his little brother would hate him for the rest of his life.

Still silent, Itachi beckoned with his hand. Not suspicious in the slightest, Sasuke trotted over. As if to check that force, Itachi jabbed him in the forehead with his index and middle fingers.

"Sorry, Sasuke. Maybe next time."

"Ow!"

His little brother pursed his lips and puffed out his cheeks, and Itachi saw that his forehead was just a bit red. When he was little, it had hurt Sasuke so much when Itachi poked him; his little brother was growing up, a fact that almost pained him.

If he stayed there like that, he wouldn't be able to get up again. Steeling himself, Itachi took a step with heavy feet. And then, without looking at his little brother, he said, "I don't have time for this."

"You always say 'Sorry, Sasuke,' and jab me in the forehead. And you never have time. It's always the same story."

Itachi left his grumpy brother, and opened the front door. *Sorry, Sasuke,* he apologized from the bottom of his heart, the moment he crossed the threshold.

∞

The cliff where I promised Shisui…

Six hours had already passed with him sitting on the edge in contemplation. No matter how he chased his thoughts off, the ideas that appeared one after another would not go away. Moments from the twelve years of his life flickered into existence and disappeared, disappeared and flickered again.

Memories of his boyhood when all he wanted was to get stronger. Days fighting as a ninja, troubled by the conflict between his comrades and his brethren. And the many bonds that dragged him into the darkness.

Beyond good and evil, beyond emotion, his memories became confused and washed away his thoughts like a muddy stream. Itachi could only give himself over to the torrent. It was too late for regret now. Still, it wasn't as though his feelings were crystal clear, either.

The karma Itachi would be burdened with was not something simple that could easily be reasoned away. It was something that went beyond preparation, worry, hesitation, determination, all of it. Which was why Itachi himself couldn't predict what kind of person he would be once that day was over. The only thing he knew for certain was that this day, "today," would indeed end, and that when it did, everyone in the clan other than his little brother would be dead.

Almost like how everyone knew that the day of their own death would come at some point.

"Haah..." Itachi took a deep breath, and let it out slowly. Through his slightly open eyelids, light the color of sunset shone into a field of view blanketed by long eyelashes.

It was almost time. The preparations had already all been made. Once Itachi moved, Madara would also move.

There was no one other than the people of the clan in the compound that day. It was a clever bit of work from Danzo and the Foundation. And dressed as that work was in the disguise of chance, no one noticed Danzo's trickery.

And it wasn't just one trick.

First, the early return of the Military Police Force. Starting that evening, contractors were coming in to build the new facilities for the headquarters, so an order was issued by the village for the police to go home early. Naturally, this was a fake order devised by Danzo. But dead men tell no tales. If everyone involved were dead, then there would be no one to say a fake order had been issued. And for the police, who had a coup d'état

the next day to consider, getting to go home early was a nice turn of events.

And the final trick...

That was to make his brother return home late. That day, a teacher at the academy would be training with him in shuriken. This teacher was a fake, a member of the Foundation. In a disguise so clever Sasuke, who was not yet even a genin, would never be able to see through it, the Foundation ninja would deceive him.

The table was set so that all Itachi had to do was head toward the compound.

"All right, I'm going," Itachi announced to empty space, as he stood up. He saw a vision of Shisui before him.

It would all end that day. The fate of the Uchiha clan, and Itachi's peaceful life...

∞

Itachi held his breath, and listened to the bright voices from across the hall. The room illuminated by the flickering glow was the dining room. The voices were those of two women. He knew one of them very well. The other was her mother.

He kicked the garbage can at his feet, and deliberately made some noise.

"What was that?" the voice he knew asked the mother.

"I don't know."

"I'll go look, all right?" Tension crept into her voice as she announced this to her mother, and then her aura slowly approached Itachi.

So that she wouldn't sense him, he ran down the hallway, and hid in the room next door. And then, once he judged that her aura had passed by him, he slipped into the dining room, and before the mother had a chance to shout upon noticing him, he knocked her out with the sharingan. Once he had soundlessly put her to sleep, he waited silently for the aura to return.

"Mom, it was just the garbage—" Having gotten this far, Uchiha Izumi stopped herself. "Itachi?" Glancing over at her mother on the floor, Izumi stared dumbfounded, not understanding what was going on. "Wh-why…"

He couldn't stand to listen to Izumi's voice any further. He concentrated his chakra in his eye. The Mangekyo sharingan.

"Tsukuyomi."

Izumi froze in place.

Itachi focused his thoughts on his own genjutsu. Tsukuyomi allowed him to completely control time, space, and matter. It was a power he had gained when he activated the Mangekyo sharingan. The time that passed within this genjutsu was one one-hundredth of one one-thousandth of one one-millionth of that of the real world.

Itachi drew out a clear image. Peace in the village of Konoha, the clan tranquil. His own form, freed from all trouble.

And Izumi beside him, smiling.

∞

Izumi becomes a chunin, as if chasing after him. At that time, Itachi is already a jonin.

He hands a pouting Izumi an engagement ring.

Izumi retiring as a ninja.

Marriage.

Childbirth.

Child-rearing.

The children setting out.

Izumi growing old together with Itachi.

Seventy years since they met.

The hair on both of their heads is white.

Izumi's illness.

He takes care of her.

Her last years...

The Mangekyo sharingan consumed an enormous amount of chakra, and so placed an equivalent burden on the user. Shoulders rising, Itachi took a deep breath, as if crawling up from the depths of the ocean. Before him, Izumi's knees gave out under her, and she collapsed, smiling.

Sliding over, Itachi held her up, tightly gripping her slender shoulders.

"Thank you." Izumi's voice sounded like that of an old woman past eighty years of age.

"Me, too. Thank you." He squeezed her shoulders more tightly, and could say nothing more.

With a broad smile on her face, Izumi took her last peaceful breath.

The mind and the body were indivisible. If the mind decays, the body also falls apart.

Izumi died, joyful.

After gently laying the now motionless Izumi down on the

floor, Itachi staggered to his feet. The intense expenditure of chakra made his body shake.

I decided that Izumi would be first...

By killing her himself, he wiped away the last of his hesitation—the hesitation borne of unfinished business with the clan, of bonds of emotion.

"Thank you, Izumi." Itachi slowly turned around. There lay her mother, knocked unconscious by the sharingan.

∞

When he stepped out of Izumi's house and onto the road, the space behind him abruptly shimmered.

"So you've begun?" Madara said evenly.

Itachi didn't look back over his shoulder at the man, but simply felt his aura. The blanket of dusk was starting to fall in the sky before him. The evening star that heralded the coming of night looked excessively bright.

"I will take care of the women and children as far as possible." Madara's concern annoyed Itachi.

"I'll take the west side of the compound, you're the east. We do this just like we planned from the start."

"Don't push yourself," Madara said.

"Shut up."

"You're still young. If you take on too much darkness, it will break you."

I've already been broken for a long time...

Itachi swallowed the words that popped into his head and turned around to look at Madara. There was no way to know

what emotion was on that face, covered as it was by a mask. His body, cloaked in a black coat that reached his shins, exuded a sinister chakra that resembled bloodlust.

"You don't need to worry about me."

"I'm not worried. It's a natural arrangement to properly execute our mission."

"Don't patronize me."

"It's precisely because I think so highly of you that I do not want you to expend excessive effort. My role, given my ability to use time and space ninjutsu, should be to take on the women and children, who will cry and shout and run about. I do think that will prioritize efficiency?"

They had to finish everything before Sasuke returned to the compound. He didn't have time to glare at Madara here.

"Whatever you want."

"I'll see you again once it's all over," Madara said, and disappeared into empty space.

Itachi took a small breath. *Close your eyes...* He moved forward in the darkness, seeking a new target.

∞

Inabi's wife died before she even understood what was happening. Shaking off the blood that wet the blade of his sword, Itachi turned his eyes to his gasping target, Inabi.

"D-do you understand what you're doing?" Inabi shot off foolishly.

Without replying, Itachi slowly closed the distance between them. With each step he took, Inabi retreated.

"How about you just prepare yourself?" Itachi suggested gently, and Inabi shook his head from side to side. "What are you afraid of? It's only the inevitable coming to you now."

"Tr-traitor."

"You all always distance yourself from everything like that. And that's why you're about to be killed by me, like this." He kicked powerfully at the floor. The distance between them closed.

Inabi tried to weave signs. Fire Style.

Too late.

Before the flames could gush out of his pointed lips, Inabi lost his own head.

∞

Itachi put his hand on the front door. Inside the now-quiet house, only one chakra shimmered.

At the end of the hallway. There was an aura in the room at the very end of the hallway. He put his hand on the sliding door.

"Who's there?" He heard the voice from inside the room, and slid the door open. "You?"

The man was sitting upright, grim look on the face that stared at Itachi. The black spot on his forehead was unmistakably Tekka's. "Chakra is shaking all over the compound. So you're the culprit, Itachi?"

Even among the Uchiha, Tekka was a leading sharingan user, and his ability to sense chakra was excellent. It wasn't at all strange that he had shrewdly grasped that some calamity had befallen the village.

"You're here. So why does chakra still shake elsewhere?"

"This isn't the time to be worrying about that."

"I see."

"Why didn't you move, if you sensed something strange in the village?"

"You got here before I could. That's all." Tekka moved to stand up.

Knife in hand, Itachi stepped in close. The man rose up, and caught Itachi in his gaze.

Sharingan.

Without flinching, Itachi squarely accepted the surge of chakra emitted by Tekka's eyes.

"Wha—" Shock crept onto the face of his target. He appeared surprised that his visual jutsu didn't work. And then, in the next instant, he saw the pattern in Itachi's eyes, and the look on his face changed to one of chagrin. "I-impossible! Mangekyo!"

Tekka's stomach swallowed Itachi's blade. He thrust it in deeply, all the way to the hilt guard. No blood gushed out, not with the sword still in place. Their faces were so close that their noses were almost touching.

"You all have the bad habit of underestimating your opponent's abilities."

"Itachi..." Blood flowed out from between Tekka's clenched teeth.

As Itachi leapt back, he yanked his sword free. An ocean of blood wet the tatami mats; he was not caught by even a drop of splash-back.

Right hand thrust up, clawing at empty space, Tekka collapsed. "Th-they won't forgive you, Itachi." Those were Tekka's last words.

Itachi turned his back on the body, and sheathed his sword. "I wasn't asking for forgiveness."

∞

In the single room of the one-person apartment, there wasn't even a bed; the small room didn't have the feel of having been lived in at all. A man sat with his back against one wall.

"Just hurry up and kill me, Team Leader."

From his careless manner of speaking, Itachi knew the man blanketed in darkness was Mezu. Anyone who looked at him would only see Uchiha Kagen.

Itachi dragged heavy feet to stand in front of him.

"You don't kill me, and everything you've done so far'll be meaningless. Nothing to get hung up on—just hurry up, and finish me off."

"Are you all right with that?"

"I've been ready for it since the time Lord Danzo took us in." A sad smile spread across Mezu's face, formerly Kagen's. "And a little brother, you always want to be useful to your big brother, you know?"

Itachi plunged his blade into the chest of the still-smiling Mezu, without so much as flinching.

∞

It had already been an hour since he put Izumi to sleep. He had murdered too many of his brethren to count, but Itachi still kept running.

His heart had long since frozen over. He had also forgotten to keep in mind that it was all for the sake of the village. He simply continued to single-mindedly swing his sword.

The target's father and mother, and then his wife. When the boy, old enough to have just started at the academy, stopped moving, he heard a shriek behind him. The voice was familiar.

The man fled down the hallway, the sound of his feet almost exaggeratedly loud. He jumped down into the entryway, and ripped open the door.

Itachi went after him. He came out onto the road.

The man looked awkward in flight. His throat stiff with fear, perhaps, he didn't even scream. Although there was already no one else left in the area. He could cry out all he wanted, but no one would hear him.

The man slipped through a stone gate on the edge of the road. Beyond it was a park. Playground equipment was set out on the square site. The man pushed past the swings so desperately, it was almost pitiable; he had made it to the center of the open space, when he fell headfirst.

Itachi stood a sword-length ahead of him, looking down on the man as he tried to find his feet. "Give up."

The man's white hair shook at Itachi's cool words. Yashiro.

"K-killing me won't solve anything, you know. There's another leader. Even Lord Fugaku doesn't know about him. I was being controlled."

"Even now, at this late stage, you're still trying to hide in someone else's shadow?"

"You have to believe me. I was just trying to do what he wanted. He's the one who—" Yashiro's eyes grew wide and froze on a spot behind Itachi. "Y-you…"

"Been a while, hm? Although I guess I did just see you two days ago."

Yashiro began trembling, eyes still fixed on Madara. "Why?"

Madara laughed, exasperated at the childish question. "Don't call me for this sort of trivial thing, Itachi."

They had decided in advance on a way to join up in an emergency. If Itachi kept an image of Madara in mind and emitted chakra, Madara would use his space-time ninjutsu, and appear before him.

"Sorry, but I chose Itachi. That's all," Madara said smoothly, and it appeared that Yashiro, still gaping up at him, had lost the will to say anything further. "Well, it's probably no use, but you should try to resist as best you can."

"H-hold on a—"

"I'll leave the rest to you. I'm going to keep working," Madara said to Itachi, and disappeared once more into thin air.

"The feeling when something you believed was absolute is made to crumble. Do you understand it a little too, now?"

"Hngh!"

Because of these men, Shisui had despaired for the clan, lost everything, and died. *I hope this at least can be comfort to you*, Itachi said to his friend.

"So, what are you going to do?" he asked, thinking it was pointless to ask, even as he waited for Yashiro's answer. If Yashiro were the kind of man who would acknowledge his own crimes, he wouldn't struggle so vainly like this.

"I-I really do understand how you feel. We'll call off the coup d'état. S-so please…"

"Begging for your life?"

"Please! Itachi! Uchiha Itachi!"

Yashiro was beyond pathetic. He was conceited enough to think he could stop the coup at his own discretion. If he hadn't been spurred on by Madara, the clan might have been able to go down a different path. When Itachi thought about this, a desire to kill so powerful it was strange even to him rose up in his heart.

"Stand up." Itachi's voice was emotionless, and Yashiro looked up at him, opening his narrow eyes as wide as possible. "You're a ninja. How about standing up and fighting?"

Yashiro said nothing.

"Have you forgotten your pride?"

Trying to somehow rein in his fear, Yashiro yanked himself to his feet, shaking his head all the while. "Don't underestimate me."

"Show, don't tell. How about you just come at me already?" Itachi said flatly, while before him, Yashiro's eyes shone red.

Not moving to defend himself, Itachi looked straight at the sharingan.

Yashiro's chakra became a spider's thread called "visual jutsu," and raced into Itachi's body.

"Fire Style!" Yashiro shouted, took a very deep breath, and puffed out his cheeks. He panicked when nothing but air came out.

"What happened to the fire?"

"Huh?!" Yashiro cried out in honest surprise.

Itachi watched coolly. "You make my movements dull with the sharingan, and release Great Fireball Technique. Because you probably anticipate that I'll leap out of the way, you bring me down in that defenseless moment with a kunai or something. Once you get the drop on me, now it's time for close combat, so you use your sharingan one more time, and get one step ahead. That's about it, right?"

He took a step toward Yashiro, who was rooted to the spot.

"Being good at getting along in the world and being good at being a ninja are two totally different things."

"Ah, ah, ah." Unable to produce words, Yashiro simply stood still, and waited for the approaching Itachi.

"Your brain was so controlled by fear that you didn't even realize you were caught in my visual jutsu when you fell."

Hearing this, Yashiro became aware for the first time that Itachi's eyes were colored crimson.

"I told you to fight so you could truly feel your own powerlessness."

"Ah, aah." Saliva drooled out of Yashiro's open mouth.

"You misjudged me to the bone." Itachi's sharingan changed. Mangekyo. "Tsukuyomi."

The second Mangekyo sharingan of that night invited Yashiro into an unnatural darkness. Crucified on a cross standing in the center of a dark ocean, he whirled his head around in confusion.

The surface of the dark water rose up at points all over, and these gradually took on human form. Infinite Itachis. In their hands, they gripped ninja swords.

"This is a world I control," Itachi murmured, his hand stretching out toward Yashiro.

"Ngaaah!"

His blade plunged into Yashiro's stomach. The Itachi who thrust it disappeared into the dark ocean.

"I won't let you die so easily."

One blade after the next pierced Yashiro's body. He became a silver hedgehog, and went limp, motionless. As Itachi returned to the ocean, the swords disappeared from Yashiro's body. A look of relief rose up onto his face, until a herd of Itachis once more blanketed his field of view.

"The real pain starts now."

Yashiro's stiff face was transformed into a smile that was already beyond terror.

Over a span of time that wasn't even a few seconds in the real world, the two faced each other silently. That moment would have seemed like several days to Yashiro. In the genjutsu space produced by the Mangekyo sharingan, swords were endlessly plunged into his body, over and over. By the time he was released to the real world, Yashiro's mind was destroyed.

"D-death...D-d-d..." Yashiro trembled and grinned.

Itachi looked down on him, as he slowly drew his sword.

Yashiro was already beyond the capacity to hear his voice. And Itachi had nothing he could say to him at this stage.

His sword flashed mercilessly, and the pitiful man's head flew up into the moonlit sky.

∞

Itachi returned to the area near the entrance to the compound. There was just one family in the Uchiha compound left alive. Only Uchiha Fugaku's family...

Sasuke would be back soon. Although he felt the pressure to hurry, Itachi turned the feet that should have returned him to his house toward the entrance to the compound. He squatted on top of an electrical pole, and looked down at the world. He could clearly see the compound's large front gates from there.

Behind them, the moon was full, almost frighteningly large. Devoid of any sense of people, the town was wrapped in silence. He could hear a crow cawing off in the distance. The melancholy echo called up the image of a raven separated from its group, drifting.

Someone slipped through the front gates. A boy carrying a bag on his shoulder. His beloved younger brother.

I should have talked so much more with him, Itachi thought, as he watched his brother running below him. He had so many things he wanted to say. Exactly how much of it would he be able to tell his little brother? One or two—no, he couldn't tell him a single thing about the truth.

In amongst all the uncountable words in his heart, Itachi felt there was just one thing that he absolutely had to tell his brother.

Locking away in his heart the feelings he could not give voice to, Itachi flew toward his own house, leaving his little brother racing along the road home.

∞

There were two auras in the room. As if lured by them, Itachi walked down the familiar hallway without taking his shoes off. Immediately after opening the door, he saw the figures of his

parents sitting together.

He stood behind them soundlessly.

"I see. So you sided with them," his father said in a controlled voice, without turning around. In his voice was a philosophical tone, as though he had understood everything.

"Dad..." Itachi was surprised at himself for automatically calling his father that. He had called him "Father" since the time he graduated from the academy. It was a distinction he drew for himself as a full-fledged ninja. And then, that name had gradually become natural, and he forgot even that he had ever called him "Dad."

Why would he use that old way of referring to his father now?

When I was little...

Back then, when there weren't the obligations of the clan, the contradiction of the village, the loneliness, the discouragement; back when his feelings about his family could be simple, might have been the happiest time in Itachi's life. And now that the parting with his family was before him, he was yearning for those old days.

"Mom..."

"We understand, Itachi." Her voice was kind, understanding everything, and still trying to envelop him in a hug.

"Itachi," his father said. "Promise me one thing." His voice was straightforward, containing not a hint of resentment. "Take care of Sasuke."

They both understand everything...

He felt it instinctively, and the feelings he had suppressed since parting with Izumi bubbled back to life. His father and mother understood everything: how much Itachi had suffered and struggled, and also the fact that this had most certainly not been an easy decision. On top of that, they were going to quietly accept the fate that had befallen them.

His father hadn't the slightest intention of crossing blades with his son. And if his father *had* turned his sword on him, his mother would have given her own life to protect Itachi. The love they felt for the son who was about to kill them radiated from them.

Why didn't I realize it sooner…

Why did it have to come to this…

He had decided that he would not regret anything, he was supposed to have readied himself, and yet the figures of his mother and father pained Itachi's heart so much he could hardly stand it.

"I will…" Tears spilled out of his eyes, and wet his cheeks. The hand holding his ninja sword shook.

"Don't be afraid. This is the path you decided on."

In the back of Itachi's mind, the conversation he'd had with his father right after he joined the Anbu—their first in a long time—came back to life.

"You should stay true to your thinking. Fight, be confused, be lost, and come through that to find your answer. And once you find it, make your decision, and do not waver from it. Find your answer, and be ready to follow through. That is determination."

"Determination…"

"Yes. There are few people in this world who live their lives with their own determination. They leave their decisions to others, and avert

their eyes from responsibility. You must not live like that at least. Move forward in your life, making your own decisions."

This was the difficult, painful path he had decided on. He must not be afraid. That had been his father's teaching.

"Compared with you, our pain will end in an instant." His father was faced with death, and yet, was thinking about the life his son would lead after this. It was as though he were trying to teach Itachi with his own life just what love was.

"Maybe I was too hasty," his father admonished himself. "I should have believed in you more. Perhaps I should have believed in you, got the clan in check, and waited."

"Dad?" His voice was shaking with his tears. His mother and father had probably noticed that he was crying. The tears were the first he'd ever let anyone else see.

"You might have been the first Uchiha Hokage. You could have wiped away even the darkness of the clan, broken through the prejudice of the village, and forged a destiny with your own power—" His father cut himself off. Itachi could tell from his shaking back that he was trying to get his emotions under control. "I stole your future from you."

Itachi couldn't find anything to say in response. Or rather, if he said anything, his feelings would break completely free.

"But it's too late for anything now." His father took a deep breath through his nose. "Even if we think differently, I'm proud of you."

My father's pride...

He had wanted to hear those words out in the sunlight. How happy would he have been to be wearing the Hokage's hat in front of the people of the village, and hear that from his proudly smiling father?

Another dream that won't come true now...

He couldn't waste any more time. His little brother was coming home.

He thrust the sword into his mother's back. A jolt of intense pain raced through Itachi's heart.

Pulling the sword out, he turned the tip toward his father.

"You're actually such a gentle child."

He lowered his head and leaned into his father, as if to press his face to that broad back. Almost like a child begging for a piggyback ride.

Now that he thought about it, his father had never spoiled him like that.

Itachi had never been selfish and troubled him, and he had never been spoiled or cried, either.

If only I had spent more time with him. Tears spilled endlessly from Itachi's eyes. Without mercy, they continued to wet the hand clutching the sword.

The slight vibrations that were coming to him through the blade stopped completely. Once he felt that his father's life had ended, he slowly pulled out his sword. Even at a time like this, he was thinking about blood spattering. He hated the Itachi that had the mindset of the ninja dyed into the marrow of his bones.

His hand wouldn't stop shaking, but he managed to somehow get the sword back in its sheath.

One final job was left. Itachi wiped away his tears, and waited for the moment.

7

The sound of footsteps racing down the hallway stopped outside the door. "Father! Mother!" his brother shouted.

"Sasuke...You must not come in!" the father he had thought was dead shouted to the other side of the door. And then this time, he really did stop moving.

The door slowly opened. Spotting the figures of his mother and father collapsed on the ground, Sasuke flew into the room.

"Father!! Mother!!"

Itachi showed his brother a face hidden by the moonlight.

His little brother's face was damp with sweat, and his eyes were twisted in fear. "Itachi!"

Sasuke took a step on trembling legs, and began to speak desperately, spreading both arms wide. "Itachi!! Itachi!! Father and Mother are—!! How?! Why?! Who would do such a—"

Itachi flung a kunai into the door behind Sasuke.

"Ngh!" A narrow cut appeared on the boy's shoulder, exposed by the rip in his clothes.

"Foolish little brother..." His final job. He would never be allowed to go back now.

Mangekyo sharingan...

"Aaaaah!!"

Father...

Blood spray.

Mother...

Itachi...

The Uchiha crest ripped apart.

Two people covered in blood…

All the hatred he would leave behind, so his brother could live.

Crawling on the ground, almost licking it, Sasuke turned just his face toward Itachi. "Why…did you…?"

"To measure my capacity."

"…Measure your capacity? You…You killed them for that?"

"I had to."

"What's…" Power came back to his little brother's body. "What's wrong with you?!"

Unable to move properly after being caught by the Mange-kyo sharingan, Sasuke simply leaned forward as if to start running, and fell over. Before him was the face of their father, the spark of life gone.

In that instant, his little brother got up, and flew from the room. He ran out of the house, and fled onto the street.

Fleeing showed an attachment to life. It was proof of a desire to live.

Finish it…

He stood in front of his brother.

"It's not true. My brother wouldn't do this. Because—"

"Pretending to be the kind of brother you hoped for…was to determine your ability."

Live.

"You will be an opponent to test my abilities. You have that potential in you."

Live.

"You felt anger and hatred toward me. You've always hoped to surpass me, so I'll let you live."

Live.

"...For my sake."

Live.

"Just like me, you have the power to awaken the Mangekyo sharingan. But there's a catch."

Sasuke stayed silent.

"You have to...kill your closest friend."

Sasuke's eyebrows shot up.

"Just as I did..."

Sasuke's eyebrows threatened to shoot off his forehead.

Live.

"That was you...You killed Shisui?!"

"And now I have the eyes."

Live.

"In the main hall of Nakano shrine...Under the seventh tatami mat from the far right, there's a secret clan meeting place."

"What?!"

"There, you'll find the *true secret* of why the visual jutsu of the Uchiha clan exists, and for what purpose."

Sasuke's face was full of questions.

"If you awaken it, then there will be *three* people who have the Mangekyo sharingan, including me. If that happens...heh, heh. Then I'll be right in letting you live."

Live.

"Right now..."

Sasuke looked alarmed.

"You are not even worth killing."

Live.

"Baby brother, you're pathetic."

Survive.

"If you want to kill me, settle for hating me! Hate me and live like the coward you are! Clinging to life without honor!"

Please.

"And someday, when you have the same eyes as I, come to me."

Live through this reality that I'm leaving you...

Trembling, his brother collapsed as though his strings had been cut.

Sasuke stuck his right leg out to brace himself, the eyes he looked at his older brother with filled with a crimson light.

Awakening.

And so, Sasuke gained another power to live. The timing was appropriate.

Itachi leapt up into the sky, about to disappear.

"Stop!!" His little brother flew up into the sky after him, and threw the three kunai that had appeared in his hand at some point.

Itachi held his breath at that sharpness. He dodged two. But he couldn't completely get out of the way of the last one. He tilted his head slightly, and took it on his forehead protector; the force of the kunai undid the knot where it was tied. The kunai plunged into the ground, and Itachi's forehead protector tumbled down next to it.

As his little brother charged him from behind, breathing hard, shoulders heaving, Itachi slowly picked up his forehead protector. Already using up the last of his strength, Sasuke wouldn't be able move from the spot.

But Itachi didn't have the luxury of worrying about the

positioning of his forehead protector. With the Konoha mark facing off to the right, he tied it roughly. He wanted to get away from there as soon as possible.

Because Itachi was crying.

His feelings, supposedly frozen, were shaken by the figure of his little brother desperately, clumsily, awkwardly clinging to him. Sasuke was mustering every last ounce of strength he had to try and stop his big brother; Itachi loved this Sasuke so much he could hardly stand it. He even had the impulse to run away with him. But under no circumstances could he do that.

Sasuke had to walk in a place where the sun reached as a ninja of the village. Itachi's life from that point on would be in the darkness. They would never live in the same place again. Not until Itachi's final days. Only then would a chance meeting in their lives be permitted.

The hero who killed his older brother, an evil criminal, and took vengeance for their clan. *That* was the glory that Sasuke would be given. For that purpose, Itachi would come face to face with his little brother one more time.

He would be killed by his brother. That was the form of Itachi's death. To that end, he could not allow Sasuke to see him crying.

He pressed his forehead protector onto his head, and steeled himself.

Farewell for now.

Itachi's body moved faster than his thoughts. Before he knew it, his little brother was in his field of view. At that moment, he understood for the first time that he was looking back. His desire to burn the image of his brother into his mind had moved his body.

But that was another thing he could not be permitted.

A mistake...

Because Itachi could feel the hot tears streaming down his cheeks. He quickly turned away from his brother, and resumed his jump. The aura of Sasuke collapsing behind him, he leaped into the moonlit night, not bothering to wipe away his tears.

The full moon, full of such beauty he wanted to rip it to pieces, was so hateful to Itachi he could hardly stand it.

∞

Not even an hour had passed since Itachi's departure, when the Anbu convened in the village to collect the bodies.

Danzo walked down a road covered in corpses. He had just left Hiruzen. Upon learning of Itachi's evil act, the Hokage was furious, and he turned the brunt of that on Danzo. Before he made it out of the Hokage's office, he had been dismissed as councilor, and made to promise to dissolve the Foundation.

But now that the tragedy of the annihilation of the Uchiha clan had been achieved, there was no reason for him to cling to the role of councilor. And even if the Foundation were officially dismantled, it was still more than possible for them to go underground and maneuver in secret, away from Hiruzen's eyes. In the end, Danzo got what he wanted.

"Lord Danzo!" A man wearing a fox mask with red markings on it.

"What's wrong, Gozu?" Danzo called his subordinate by name.

Gozu was silent.

The instant he saw the two openings in the mask hidden under a hood, Danzo gasped.

Red eyes with a pattern like three magatamas mixed together in the center...

"You!"

"I'll always be watching," Itachi—dressed as Gozu—said. "If you lay a hand on Sasuke, I'll leak all the village's secrets to enemy lands."

"You should know what that will bring down upon the village, Itachi."

"I'm outside the village now."

"I thought you were a capable pawn... It does seem that I misjudged you."

"If you lay a hand on Sasuke, I will destroy you. Carve that into your soul." Itachi turned into countless crows, and vanished.

"Don't take your eyes off of him," Danzo muttered to no one; in his ears, he heard the sound of insect wings.

∞

"Sneaking all the way in here without anyone noticing. You really are a capable ninja." The third Hokage, Sarutobi Hiruzen, smiled as he sat up in his futon. "So, I suppose you determined that no one will be able to hear us in here?"

"Yes," Itachi replied, kneeling in front of the futon.

"I've already marked your name down in the Bingo Book as an S-rank criminal. You shouldn't be able to infiltrate the village, much less sneak all the way into my bedroom. Will you tell me what you wanted to talk with me about that you would go to such lengths?"

"It's about Sasuke."

"No need to worry. That child's done nothing wrong. We will take care of him as one of the children of the village."

The Hokage's strong words eased Itachi's heart. "Thank you. But..."

"Is it Danzo?"

"Yes." Itachi was grateful to the Hokage's powers of insight, as sharp as the sharingan. On the other hand, he also hated them.

If Hiruzen was so gifted at reading the minds of others, then why couldn't he have managed to find a way to cooperate with the Uchiha clan? Itachi did have the urge to press the older man about the issue, but he knew it would do no good thinking about that now.

It wouldn't change the fact that Itachi was an S-rank criminal. The entire Uchiha clan, with the exception of the brothers, Itachi and Sasuke, was destroyed. That was reality.

"No need to worry about Danzo. He's been formally dismissed as councilor, and I also ordered him to disband the Foundation."

"Will he meekly follow orders?"

"He has already stepped down as councilor. The Foundation has been disbanded, on the surface. But I cannot deny the possibility that he is cultivating it in secret somewhere. I ordered the people who were watching the Uchiha clan to monitor him now."

There was no longer any need to monitor the Uchiha clan. The third Hokage's words dug into Itachi's heart.

"Fear not, Itachi. I will not allow him to lay a finger on Sasuke."

"I appreciate that." Itachi bowed his head deeply. "Well, then..." He stood up, and turned his back to the Hokage.

"What will you do now?"

"There's an organization I'm interested in," Itachi replied, eyes still on the door.

"So, you'll join them?"

"Yes. I'll watch them from the inside, and if it looks like they're going to act out, I will do whatever I have to to stop them."

"Even leaving the village, you are still more than anything a ninja who loves peace, hm?"

Itachi felt that he was still a ninja of Konoha, even then. The village of Konohagakure, where Sasuke lived, was Itachi's home. Even if he wanted to abandon it, he could not.

"What's the name of this organization?"

"Akatsuki..."

∞

"How about you show yourself?" Itachi muttered to no one in the middle of the deserted woods. His voice had not even faded away, when a small flame flickered to life in the empty space. It burned ferociously for a moment, before quickly growing smaller and disappearing. Only a faint scattering of ashes remained. Among the ashes dancing in midair was a piece of a transparent wing. "You're here, aren't you? Aburame man."

"I CALLED MYSELF SUGARU BEFORE YOU, YES?"

A myriad of small winged insects came together in the forest, where there had previously been nothing, to create an enormous dark form in empty space. The buzzing of their wings layered together to form words that reached Itachi's ears.

"You're not interested in giving up on watching me, and going back to your master?"

"YOU ALSO UNDERSTAND THAT SUCH A THING WOULD NOT BE PERMITTED, DON'T YOU?"

"No, huh?"

The insects gradually took on a human shape. A man wearing a white tiger mask appeared out of the ether, and floated in midair accompanied by the sound of countless tiny wings.

"I don't plan on being Danzo's pawn forever."

"HE DOES NOT CARE ABOUT YOUR DESIRES. FOR HIM, THE MOST IMPORTANT THINGS ARE WHAT HE SHOULD DO, AND HOW HE SHOULD BE."

"So, a stalemate." Itachi looked up at Sugaru. "Then there's only one way to resolve this." His sharingan glittered.

"THAT SORT OF THING HAS NO EFFECT ON ME."

"Not on you." Itachi concentrated his chakra, and boosted his sharingan to the Mangekyo sharingan. He was conscious of the eyes of the insects in Sugaru's body, too many to count.

He felt a dull pain in his right eye. It was because he had been overusing the sharingan ever since that night.

"You said that you're always watching me. But you're only one person. You eat and sleep. So who's watching me, then?"

"NO NEED TO SPEAK IN SUCH A ROUNDABOUT MANNER... OH..."

"It seems you've noticed."

ITACHI'S STORY
[MIDNIGHT]

Something seemed to be wrong with Sugaru, floating in space. It looked like he was desperately fighting something, his body jerking and twitching.

"Did you think I hadn't noticed the insects watching over me?"

"IMPOSSIBLE... THE MANGEKYO SHARINGAN ON MY *KOCHU* INSECTS..."

"By sharing your chakra, you assimilate what the insects have seen into your own experience. It's a more effective method than Shadow Clones."

The sound of wings disappeared from within Sugaru. At the same time, his body, suddenly gaining gravity, was sucked down to the surface of the earth. Unable to control his body, Sugaru plunged into the ground headfirst, incapable of even landing.

"Ngh. Unh unh unh." Sugaru's injured vocal cords emitted a real groan.

Itachi looked down on him coolly. "This is for Shisui."

"W-WAIT..."

"Amaterasu," he murmured.

A black flame sprouted on Sugaru's shoulder. The strange blaze spread, in the blink of an eye, to swallow his entire body. As if trying to abandon their burning host, the insects fled from every hole, but they were all caught up in the dark blaze.

"This fire will not go out until whatever I'm looking at has completely burned up. I won't let even one of the insects nesting in you escape."

Sugaru's cries of agony rang out through the forest. Around him, insects buzzed and fluttered, shrouded in dark flames. They looked almost like black fireflies that bloomed in the daytime.

∞

"I still can't believe it," her former teammate said, staring into the teacup in her hand; Shinko let out a sigh, turning a sympathetic gaze her way. "I mean, that *that* Itachi would do something like that." A tear spilled out of Himuka's eyes, and a small ripple rose up on the surface of the light green liquid in her cup.

"I can't believe it, neither, but facts're facts."

"But, senpai!"

"I'm not yer senpai no more! Quit with calling me that already."

"It's just—"

"C'mon, have a dumpling and feel better." Shinko offered Himuka one of the sweet bean dumplings set out on the bench.

"Thank you," the other girl said, as she took a skewer of the tiny round treats, opened her tiny mouth as wide as she could, and stuffed a dumpling in. "It's really good," she said, smiling.

Shinko smiled back as she turned toward the road, and looked up at the sky. A single bird danced in the clear blue. It was a strange bird, carving out circles in the sky like a hawk or an eagle.

"So, like, I sorta kinda get it, ya know."

"What's that?" Himuka asked, popping another dumpling in her mouth.

"That kid mighta been six years younger 'an me, but he was way more grownup," Shinko answered, still looking up at the sky.

"I know what you mean. I mean, I'm older than him, but I just naturally ended up calling him 'Master Itachi.'"

"An' he had all kinds of annoying things he was carryin' around, so I think maybe he just reached his limit, yeah? I mean, I heard he even killed that cute girl he brought here that one time. He's not the sort of kid to do that. Not that Itachi."

If they kept talking, she'd start crying, too. Shinko desperately pushed back the hot thing welling up in her chest.

"I suppose you're right. So, he did have a girlfriend, after all," Himuka murmured, head hanging.

As if to banish her tears, Shinko turned around forcefully. "So, like, that mean you fancied Itachi, then?"

"N-no, that's—"

"Not gonna be straight with me, hm?" She sprang at Himuka, and poked her in the side.

Her former junior teammate began laughing.

Shinko murmured, too quietly to be heard, "It's all right. I get it..." She was casually wiping away the tears that leaked from her eyes once more, when she heard the voice of the owner calling from inside the shop.

Whatever happened, life still went on.

∞

"Did you take care of that little annoyance?"

Itachi nodded silently at the man sitting on the enormous stump. They were on a rocky mountain near the border between nations. The trees around them were neatly felled, revealing the bare earth. The wind gusted ceaselessly across the desolate landscape. Withstanding these gusts that threatened to blow him away, Itachi stood facing the man in the mask.

"So, then, what will you do?" The mask covering the man's face, patterned after a vortex, turned toward Itachi. The round hole in the area of the man's right eye stared at him.

Uchiha Madara.

"I'm an S-rank criminal. No matter where I go, people will be after me."

"Did you think about what we talked about before? I should think it would be quite convenient to protect a wanted man like you."

"Right..."

"I'll introduce you to a truly interesting man," Madara said, and turned his face toward empty space.

"Right. Call him." He appeared to be talking with someone via chakra. "It's been a while, hm? There's just someone I want you to meet. Right. Oh, go through Pain, and send your chakra here. Align your chakra with Pain."

Madara looked at Itachi once more. "He's here."

A rainbow-colored wave rose up in the nothingness next to the stump Madara was sitting on. It shimmered and shook fiercely for a while, but then gradually took on the shape of a human, until finally becoming the clear figure of a man. A man Itachi had seen before.

"Oh my, it's been a while, hm, Itachi?" the rainbow-colored vision uttered in a creepy voice that sent a chill up his spine.

"You..." Itachi murmured.

Madara raised his voice. "One of the legendary Sannin... Orochimaru."

"Strange for you to be so sarcastic about it." The corners of the rainbow phantom's mouth curled up slightly.

"Perhaps I'm a little overexcited at the situation."

"Heh, heh, heh. That's not like you."

"I suppose."

As he listened to this conversation between the two, carried on in the familiar tones of old friends, Itachi's thoughts drifted elsewhere.

Orochimaru was a serious criminal who performed forbidden experiments on people before he was chased out of the village by the third Hokage. And together with Jiraiya and Tsunade, he had been named a "legendary Sannin" in the Second Shinobi World War, where he had been feared by many ninjas. Uchiha Madara was a ninja of legend from the founding of Konohagakure. Both were so powerful that there wasn't a ninja in the world who didn't know their names. And these two had joined and maneuvered in secret with the organization Akatsuki. What on earth were they planning?

He couldn't simply let this go.

"We met any number of times while I was in the village. I suppose it's been nine years then, Itachi."

He hadn't been particularly close with the man. Back when Orochimaru was still in the village, Itachi knew him well enough to say hello. They were not friendly enough for the intimate way Orochimaru spoke to him.

"You left the village six years ago."

"Oh my, is that so? I've been reborn once since then. Using forbidden jutsu, of course."

Orochimaru had been doing experiments on people from the time he was in the village, so Itachi wasn't especially surprised that he had managed to be reborn.

"This jutsu, in exchange for offering the user eternal time, slightly dulls your perception of time. You've had the experience of not being sure if you ate a certain meal yesterday or the day before that, haven't you? For me, ten years is no different from ten days ago."

Itachi stayed silent.

"Heh, heh. None of that matters, though, does it? This man brought you and I together for an altogether different reason, yes?" The phantom's lips stretched out to the sides, like a snake's mouth. "If you were to join Akatsuki, I too would find it heartening."

"Are there any other ninjas who were in Konohagakure?"

"Me and this man, and if you join, that will be just three."

"I see." From Orochimaru's words, he assumed there were also ninjas from other villages in Akatsuki.

A darkness was beginning to squirm in a place beyond the villages.

"That village could only maintain its peace by eliminating our clan. And the ninja is a creature that can only make its presence known by forcing others to yield. I wouldn't mind seeing what kind of measures they come up with against your organization."

"That answer is very you." Orochimaru laughed mysteriously.

Madara ignored him, and stood up. "Welcome to Akatsuki."

Itachi took the proffered right hand. It was frightfully cold, a hand in which no trace of blood could be felt, so cold he almost wondered if the leather glove that covered it was frozen.

"All right, then. I'll take my leave. We'll meet again, Itachi." The phantom of Orochimaru disappeared into thin air.

"Shall we go, then?"

"Where?"

"First, the village of Amegakure, where our base is." Madara's eyes, peering out from behind his mask, shone red.

Suddenly, Danzo's words came back to life in Itachi's mind: *"Chaos will follow you throughout your life."*

At that moment, Itachi was about to step into the vortex of the people trying to create chaos. That night, he had lost the light of hope, along with his clan.

Be the best ninja, ascend to Hokage, use that position freely to lead the world to peace, and then...

Rid this world of all fighting.

That was the path of hope he had envisioned. He had lost everything.

But.

Even if hope was lost, the dream remained. Even if he didn't walk down the path of hope, he could still chase after his dream of ridding the world of fighting. If he was the possessor of bad luck, then so be it. If it was Itachi's destiny to constantly call chaos, he would use that to his full advantage.

He would draw all the fighting and disaster and hatred of people in this world into his heart. He trusted that he would be able to realize his dream by positioning himself in the center of the vortex. Fight, fight, fight through, and beyond that...

His little brother awaited him. In the world of peace that would come, once he had swallowed the chaos. In the center of it stood Sasuke, the hero who struck down his older brother—the personification of great sin.

The darkness is my dream's partner... Itachi ran after Madara.

Above his head, a single bird flew, as though accompanying him. Spreading out before him was an eternal darkness. Even so, on Itachi's mouth, a divine, sublime smile rose up.

His little brother was at the end of this path.

"I'll be waiting for you, Sasuke."

Itachi's last journey was beginning.

Was the world truly saved by sealing away Otsutsuki Kaguya?

No, it wasn't. If the Infinite Tsukuyomi was released, and people returned to their old way of living again, they would no doubt make the same mistakes.

What's truly terrifying is not enormous evil. It's the little evil nesting in the hearts of people...

My older brother knew that. He bore these evils in himself, and died a criminal who wanted peace more than anyone else.

So then, what should I do?

Only the truly strong can see the weakness in the hearts of people, take in their evil feelings, and continue to live despite that.

Only I can do it...

So then, I will. I'll walk down the path that my brother gave his life to show me.

"Revolution."

MASASHI KISHIMOTO

Author/artist Masashi Kishimoto was born in 1974 in
rural Okayama Prefecture, Japan. Like many kids, he
was first inspired to become a manga artist in elementary
school when he read *Dragon Ball* by Akira Toriyama. After
spending time in art college, he won the Hop Step Award
for new manga artists with his story *Karakuri*. After
considering various genres for his next project, Kishimoto
decided on a story steeped in traditional Japanese culture.
His first version of *Naruto*, drawn in 1997, was a one-shot
story about fox spirits; his final version, which debuted in
Weekly Shonen Jump in 1999, quickly became the most popular
ninja manga in the world. The series would also spawn
multiple anime series, movies, novels, video games and more.
Having concluded the series in late 2014, Masashi Kishimoto
has kept himself busy this year with the sidestory *Naruto: The
Seventh Hokage and the Scarlet Spring* and writing the story
for the latest Naruto movie, *Boruto: Naruto the Movie* both
of which will focus on the title character's son, Boruto.

TAKASHI YANO

Takashi Yano won the *Shosetsu Subaru* Newcomer Award
in 2008 with *Jashu*. He has published a number of
works since then as an expert on period dramas. He
is also active in a number of other places, including
writing the story for the *Assassin's Creed 4* manga.